SOCKS
ARE nOT
Enough

10654700

MARK LOWERY

grew up in Preston but now he lives in Cambridge. He has a real-life human girlfriend who definitely exists and a baby daughter. Most of the time he is a teacher and this is his first book.

His favourite biscuits are:

1. CHOCOLATE DIGESTIVES (DARK)
2. PARTY RINGS
3. CHOCOLATE FINGERS
4. CHOCOLATE DIGESTIVES (MILK)
5. CUSTARD CREAMS

SOCKS ARE NOT ENOUGH

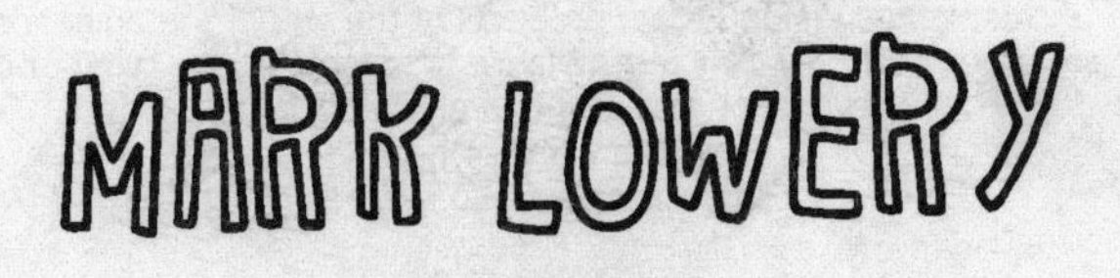

SCHOLASTIC

First published in the UK in 2011 by Scholastic Children's Books
An imprint of Scholastic Ltd
Euston House, 24 Eversholt Street
London, NW1 1DB, UK
Registered office: Westfield Road, Southam, Warwickshire, CV47 0RA
SCHOLASTIC and associated logos are trademarks and/or registered
trademarks of Scholastic Inc.

ISBN 978 1407 13104 7

A CIP catalogue record for this book is available
from the British Library.

Printed and bound by CPI Group (UK) Ltd, Croydon, CR0 4YY
Papers used by Scholastic Children's Books are made from
wood grown in sustainable forests.

1 3 5 7 9 10 8 6 4 2

www.scholastic.co.uk/zone

For S and J

Dealing With Feelings Lesson 1

Here are ten bad things that happened to me over the last three weeks. They are the reasons why I am here.

1. My parents decided to stop wearing clothes.
2. As number 1 got out of hand, they joined what can only be described as a terrorist group, hijacked a torchlit parade and shamed me in front of the whole city.
3. My idiot of a brother stole and ruined the most wonderful girl in the world.
4. I gave my brother's girlfriend a black eye (an accident).
5. I was accused of stalking my brother's girlfriend (a misunderstanding).
6. Because of number 1, my mum was arrested last Tuesday and spent the night in jail (unfortunately the incident in question was neither an accident *nor* a misunderstanding).
7. My brother got his own back for numbers 4 and 5 in a typically devious and underhanded way.
8. Because of 7, I unknowingly offended the mayor of a

small French town and caused a near riot at a swimming gala. Consequently, I was suspended from school until today and was banned from my local swimming pool for life.

9. Because of 1, I suffered the most disturbing thing I could ever have imagined. As a result, I will never eat Coco Pops again.
10. Because of 1-9, I have barely spoken for five days. I have also moved out of my house and have been living in a tent in the back garden for the last week.

As a result of items 1-10, I must now have a one hour lesson every day with Miss O'Malley. It is called "Dealing With Feelings". The school and my parents have made it clear that this class is not optional. I have to go.

There are two people in this lesson. They are:

a. Miss O'Malley (the school nurse, counsellor and student welfare coordinator).
b. Me (Michael Swarbrick).

This is the first lesson. It is held in Miss O'Malley's office. After walking in at the start of the lesson, I sat opposite Miss O'Malley with her desk in between us. She then asked me a load of questions about how I was feeling. I did not answer any of them because I do not want to talk about what happened.

After what felt like about two hours of awkward silence, Miss O'Malley smiled and patted me on the wrist. I noticed at this point that Miss O'Malley has big hands; huge great hands that could crush a kitten. This is strange because she is quite small and has a voice with an Irish accent that is as gentle as a draught under a door. Those hands look out of place, like those foam fingers people wear at wrestling matches.

After removing her enormous paw from my wrist, Miss O'Malley told me that, if I preferred not to talk, I could just write about everything that was bothering me. She assured me that I could write anything I wanted and no one outside of these four walls would ever read it. She then pulled a laptop out from under her desk. She said the school had given it to her but she has never used it because she keeps everything in her noggin. At this point she tapped herself on the side of the head. As she did this, I could not take my eyes off her colossal hand. She should be more careful when she taps herself on the head. That massive thing could fracture her skull.

My mind started to wander. I wondered where she buys gloves from. They have shops for people who are incredibly tall or incredibly fat. Do they have glove shops just for ladies with big hands? It is probably too small a market really. Not many women have hands like hers. The shop would probably have to sell big shoes as well, just to stay afloat. Miss O'Malley wears Velcro shoes. I doubt she could manage to tie a shoelace with those sausage fingers.

Eventually I decided that I had to stop thinking about her hands. This seems to be a problem of mine. I become quite obsessed with certain things about how people look. For instance, I know that my so-called mate Paul Beary has a birthmark the shape of a bat under his arm and nineteen verrucas on his left foot.[1]

I booted up the laptop and started to type. After all, it is not every day that someone just gives you a laptop to use.

Privacy

Oh no! Miss O'Malley was just reading over my shoulder. Even though the room is small, I had not noticed her moving around from the other side of the desk. She read everything, even the stuff about the big hands. At first I thought she was going to be mad but do you know what she did? She smiled! Then she said, "Oh good. Very good. Write *exactly* what you're feeling. Very organized, too. Wonderful to see you using lists and footnotes. Lists are an excellent idea, Michael. They unblock feelings-congestion and clear out any thought-jams."

I like lists too. I could make a list of twenty reasons why but that would be going too far. I guess I just prefer it when things are in order. Even my clothes are alphabetized in my wardrobe

1 On the rare occasions when he does PE, I count to see if he has grown a new one.

(from a seven-year-old Action Man T-shirt to a zebra-print jumper that my mum bought me three Christmases ago and I have still never worn).

Anyway. The lesson is almost over. I guess it was not too bad. If she is not going to care if I write about her, then that means I really *can* write what I like. I will write the whole story down. I guess I might have already spoiled it by writing a list of all the best bits (or the worst bits, depending how you look at it). That is not important, though. The list does not even tell half of what happened.

Dealing With Feelings Lesson 2

This is the second day of Dealing With Feelings. There are two good things about being in this lesson today.

1. As it is a Tuesday, I get to miss art with Miss Skinner. Miss Skinner has goss eyes and a moustache. These are not reasons for disliking her. They are just facts. I do not like being in her lesson because it is uncomfortable after everything that happened. The school thought it best that I did not go into her lessons any more because of her connection with everything. I also think that this is because everyone knows art is pointless and because I am rubbish at it. I once made a car out of clay. Miss

Skinner said it was an excellent cow. A *cow*. She even praised the detail on the udders. I could not understand if this was because she is goss-eyed or because I am rubbish at art. Probably a bit of both.

2. Miss O'Malley. She is nice. This afternoon, she gave me a biscuit and some orange squash at the start of the lesson. The squash is usually for the kids who faint on hot days. She held the glass in her massive hand and poured the squash in, measuring it out carefully. "Just one finger's worth," she muttered to herself. I swear there was about half a pint of it in there before she added the water.

When I sat down, Miss O'Malley asked me some more questions like yesterday. "Anything you want to talk about today?", "How are things at home?", "Are you still living in the tent?" etc.[2] I grunted and shrugged to each one and concentrated on my biscuit, which was a fruit shortcake (best-before date probably around 1983). I washed it down with some squash. It was so strong that my teeth felt like they were about to dissolve.

Miss O'Malley nodded and said "Good, good," then pulled the laptop out of the safe where she keeps the syringes for

---

2 I have got a very sore neck from sleeping in the tent. Also, as today is the second of October, it was absolutely freezing last night. There is a real price to pay for getting away from your parents.

diabetic students. I think it was kept in there because she wanted me to know that no one could read what I had typed. I liked this thought. She then busied herself around the office, telling me to keep up the good work and to let it all pour out.

Here goes. This is my story.

Swimming

I am a swimmer.

Well, that is not quite true. I am just a person who likes swimming.

Actually that is not true either. I hate it. From the age of six until just over a week ago, I was forced by my mum to go swimming. This was completely against my will.

And every single week for the last eight and a half years, she stood on the balcony and watched me: length after boring length; session after painful session. I have no idea why she did this, as watching other people training at swimming is probably the most boring thing in the world. Despite this fact, though, she has watched every single training session I have ever been to. Apart from Saturdays.

I will soon have to write about why she never used to come on a Saturday. It is not pleasant.

Anyway, I *am* a member of a swimming club.

Or at least I *was*, before everything that happened. But I am pretty good.

Depending on who or what you compare me to, that is.

I am better at swimming than, say, a slug but much worse than a sea lion.

To be honest, in human terms, I am pretty rubbish.

There was a reason that I put up with swimming, though, despite my lack of speed, technique or enthusiasm. A brilliant, talented reason. A reason that cut through the water like a dolphin. A reason that sparkled like a ray of sunshine dancing on a coral reef.

Lucy King.

Lovely Lucy King.

Lucy King the national swimming champion and age-group record holder (100m freestyle – Under 16 age group).

Lucy King the kind, wonderful girl who, despite having just started her GCSE year *and* training for over fifteen hours per week,[3] still found time to help out with teaching swimming to some disabled kids in the learner pool twice a week.

Lucy King who once smiled at me. Fact.

---

3 Source: Preston Piranhas Swimming Club website, "Meet Our Champions Page" (memorized by me). Other facts include:
Favourite food: grilled chicken and boiled potatoes. Ambition: to compete in the Olympics. Pets: none. Favourite training drill: leg kick with flippers. Least favourite stroke: butterfly (although she does hold the club record for this stroke in all junior age groups from Under 11 upwards – I could write down all of the different times from memory but I will not). Favourite film: *Finding Nemo.* Training tip: stay focused.

Now, if anyone read this, I know exactly what they would say. They would say, "Oooh, Mike Swarbrick fancies Lucy King. Mike Swarbrick with his stupid waggly head and pot belly and skinny arms fancies The Most Beautiful Girl in Preston."[4]

They would be 100%, completely and utterly **wrong**. I do not *fancy* her. I *admire* her. There is a big difference. Paul Beary, my so-called mate, *fancies* girls. He stares at them through binoculars when they are doing PE and tries to sniff their hair in the school corridor. That is *fancying*. *Admiring* a girl is when you say, "Oh, I think that such and such is a very talented, lovely person. I had not noticed her looks at first but, since you mention it, I suppose she is quite pretty after all. Not that it matters, of course. I will find out everything I can about her so maybe we could one day be good friends. Perhaps we could eat grilled chicken and boiled potatoes together whilst watching *Finding Nemo* then afterwards discuss training regimes or I could carry her swimming bag for her or polish her flippers or something like that. But I would never, never ruin her reputation or our friendship by being the kind of boy who *fancies* her. No way. Definitely not me. I mean, why would I? Honestly."

---

4 I know this because my so-called mate Paul Beary once said these exact words to me.

Where It All Began to Go Wrong

I realize now that the problems must have been building up for years without me realizing. Like how pressure rises in a volcano for ages but people only know they are in danger when a lump of red-hot lava lands on their cat. I sometimes do not notice things that are happening right in front of my eyes. For example, one time I trapped my school tie in that thing next to the sink that grinds up leftover food. It had been mangled right up to the knot before I realized. I had to cut myself free with a potato peeler (the only thing to hand) otherwise I could have been pulped like a mouldy carrot.

Anyway, I was at training on Saturday morning just over three weeks ago. Back when I was a member of the club, Saturdays were my favourite swimming sessions. In fact, they were the only ones I enjoyed. This was because, for reasons I unfortunately learned later, Saturday was the only session that my mum did not come to watch. As a result, it was the only training session that I willingly attended.

I do not like to be watched.

The swimming club only hired two lanes as most people have better things to do at the weekend. The rest of the pool was for public swimming. One lane was reserved for the Elite Competition Squad, strictly by invitation only (the sessions were for people who had a chance of victory in forthcoming big events. Usually only Lucy King and one or two others were deemed good enough to train in it). The other lane was for Squad Development. This was a polite way of saying the Losers' Lane.

Every member of the other squads in the club was welcome to train in the Losers' Lane. Well, I say welcome. We were not really welcome at all but the club had to at least pretend it cared about all of its swimmers and not just the good ones. We were never made to feel like valued club members. We were treated more like pieces of raw sewage floating down a rat-infested pipe. This was because the session was run by Dave King, the club's head coach.

Here are some facts about Dave King:

1. He is Lucy's dad.
2. His entire body seems to be made of one giant bulging muscle and a network of veins that throb and pulsate whenever he is angry (which is often).
3. He always has a clipboard and a stopwatch hanging round his neck. Even when I have seen him going into the loo after training, he is still carrying them. I mean, what could he possibly be timing in there? Well, apart from the obvious.
4. He has a very violent temper. I once saw him pick a boy up by his goggles and throw him five metres down the pool.
5. He hates losers. This most definitely includes me.

6. He is missing three fingers on one hand. Someone once told me he used to be in the SAS and he lost his fingers in hand-to-hand combat training. I do not know if this is true but, if it is, he probably then beat his opponent to death with them soon afterwards.

The other main reason why I loved this session so much was that I was guaranteed to be in the lane next to Lucy King. I could *admire* her swimming technique from really close up. She was so close that, when she pushed off the wall, the bubbles from her nose would tickle my face. Sometimes, if she was practising leg kick, the tips of her flippers would brush against my shoulder. At other times, her hand would graze across mine and I'd think about grabbing it so we could swim down the pool together like a pair of joyful porpoises.

This never happened, though. Normally, she would streak past me at high speed and I would be left spluttering in the water, wishing that I had not left my inhaler in my bag.

Anyway, on this one particular day I had turned up for the session at 8:50 a.m., ten minutes before it was due to start.

I do not like to be late for things.

At 8:55, Dave King stalked along the poolside, stopwatch and clipboard bouncing up and down against his huge chest.

"Ready to work hard, Malcolm?" he grunted, barely looking at me as he scribbled the plan for Lucy's training session on to the whiteboard. "Not long till the Guild swimming gala. Don't want you humiliating yourself like you did at the club championships."

I smiled weakly. He was referring to the time I injured myself on a slippery diving block just before my race last year.

The rest of the pool was full of the usual types of people: old men and women swimming lengths, the odd annoying person doing widths and getting in everyone's way, and a few hyperactive boys bombing and getting told off by the lifeguards.

A couple of minutes later, Lucy wandered out of the changing rooms in her dressing gown. Her flippers, arm paddles, pull-buoy and goggles were balanced expertly on her float.

I smiled at her but she did not smile back. This is because she is very focused before training. I made a mental note not to distract her again when she is clearly in the zone. Without warning, she slipped off her dressing gown and started stretching on the poolside. I had to quickly look away, feeling my face turn red. The last thing I wanted to do was to stare at her when she was unawares. If I had been my so-called mate Paul Beary, I would have probably wolf-whistled and twanged the straps of her costume.

"Right, Luce," growled Dave King, tapping the whiteboard. He always did this when he was going into technical detail. "Today's the eighth of September. We've only got a few months till the Nationals and two weeks till the Preston Guild gala.[5] We're going all out now, Luce, so no slacking. Four hundred metres front crawl warm-up. Looking for long strokes out there. First hundred at fifty per cent, second at seventy-five, third at ninety, fourth on full race speed. Do *not* slap the water with your left hand. It cost you zero point zero five seconds a length in the regionals and could easily be the difference between a medal. . ."

"And a muddle," finished Lucy, adjusting her goggles and diving in with a tiny splash.

Dave smiled as she cut through the water like a barracuda. "That's my girl."

I stood there, shivering in the cool air as he watched her gliding down the pool, checking his stopwatch and scribbling something down on his clipboard.

Another swimmer joined Lucy's lane – a girl called Emma who has shoulders like a weightlifter's and can beat most of the boys in the club at arm wrestling. Some people call her Brutus the Beefcake behind her back. I do not think this is fair but it seems to sum her up quite well.

After a brief instruction from Dave, she dived in behind

---

5 This is part of the Preston Guild – an ancient, once-every-twenty-years celebration of the city's right to hold a market. Exciting, eh? As this is Guild year, the Preston Piranhas swimming club was to host a gala against a team from our French twin town. We would also have our own float in the torchlight procession through the city centre. Unfortunately I will have to write more about these events later.

Lucy and powered along behind her, the gap between them growing noticeably with every couple of strokes. Dave muttered something under his breath about her having all the elegance of a hippo in comparison to Lucy. This seemed to make him quite happy.

I cleared my throat. "Erm. Dave."

Dave spun round and glared at me like I'd just been scooped out of the baby pool after a nappy had burst. "What is it, Martin? Can't you see I'm busy?"

I tried to smile. "What would you like me to do?"

"Just go up and down a few times," he said, waving his hand dismissively. "Think you can handle that? Oh, and by the way, we need someone just like you for the club float at the torchlit procession. Interested?"

"Yes, please," I said, quickly. From the website, I knew that Lucy was going to play the queen of the sea and they were still looking for the king.

"Good. We need someone to dress as a sea slug. The other short, chubby-looking kid quit the club after I told him to go on a diet. Now get in and get going, you're wasting time here."

With his crazy, bulging eyes burning into my back, I quickly belly-flopped into Losers' Lane and spluttered my way through a couple of lengths. I was the only person in there.

I supposed that being a sea slug would not be so bad. I mean, I would have preferred to be the king of the sea but never mind. The website said that the sea slugs were the queen's guardians. Protecting her would be nice. I could protect her from the king of the sea and make sure he kept his salty hands off.

An Unwanted Underwater Idiot

It was on my third or fourth length that everything went wrong.

There was a commotion up ahead in Lucy's lane. She had stopped suddenly mid-stroke and was frantically treading water. Bubbles and flailing legs were everywhere. It was a bit like *Jaws*, only without the shark.

I swam up alongside her to see if she was OK. She was speechless, pointing down at the bottom of the pool with her lovely mouth hanging open. When I ducked my head underwater, I could not believe what I saw. Lying on the bottom of the pool and looking upwards at Lucy was a lad in a scuba-diving mask. A lad about my age. A lad with a large gut and a filthy grin on his stupid face. A lad who recognized me straight away and started waving madly.

"Oh no," I said out loud, the bubbles pouring out of my mouth.

It was Paul Beary – one of my so-called mates from school.

Actually that makes it sound like I have other mates. I do not. He is the only one. When you only have one friend in the world, you cannot afford to be picky.

Some things you should know about Paul Beary:

1. He is very overweight. He says that this is because he has problems with his genes. My brother, Ste, says that the only problem Paul has with genes is finding a pair that he can get past his arse.[6]
2. He is obsessed with women. Not in a good way either. Sometimes when he fancies girls, he steals their used cutlery from the slopping-out bucket in the school canteen. He then uses them to eat with because it is "just as good as snogging them".
3. He claims to have had a French girlfriend called Cherie who "showed him everything". I do not believe him. He also says that his uncle invented the caravan, that there is a cat ghost that lives in his bed and that his granddad was the first person in Britain to be called Nathan.

"What are you doing?" I mouthed to him. I was not happy

Paul drew the hourglass shape of a woman with his hands, then pointed at Lucy and gave me the thumbs up. His cheeks were puffed out from holding his breath for so long.

Lucy was treading water in her lane. As I took a breath, I looked over to her.

---

6 This is one of only two times that my brother has ever made me laugh. I felt bad straight afterwards, though, as it was at the expense of my best and only friend. However, I stopped feeling bad when Paul smacked me one in the arm for laughing.

"Do you know *that*?" she said pointing downwards, her face twisted in disgust. She was and still is the only girl in the world who can still look good when she is furious.

"Nothing to do with me!" I squeaked.

Lucy shook her head. "Pathetic."

At that point, there was a loud bellowing from the side of the pool. "Oiiii! What's goin' on in there!"

Dave King was storming down the poolside, his eyes glowing like two angry coals and his clipboard swinging wildly.

Lucy pointed down to the bottom of the pool. "Peeping Tom," she said, sounding as though it happened a lot. Knowing Paul, it probably did.

What happened next was quite spectacular. Dave King gave a roar like a gorilla, threw his clipboard and stopwatch down on the poolside and dived in fully clothed. He shot straight underneath me like a torpedo, grabbed Paul with one hand and dragged him across the pool underwater.

At the other side, he hauled Paul out by his leg, shoved him on to the floor and towered over him, snarling and waving his fists. Petrified, Paul slithered away on his belly like a walrus and legged it out into the changing room.

Everyone in the pool was staring. The old people had stopped swimming. The hyperactive kids had stopped bombing. Even the lifeguard had dropped his whistle.

"And you can get out an' all, Mario!" he yelled at me. "Distracting my athletes!"

Water was pouring from his clothes and his shirt was clinging to his huge muscles. Not wanting him to drag me out as well, I ducked under Lucy's lane. As I swam across it, I tried to say sorry about Paul but she had already resumed her length.

WHACK!

I doubled over in pain. When Brutus the Beefcake was swimming past, she booted me in the stomach with her size ten foot. I do not think it was an accident.

Dealing With Feelings Session 3

I stopped writing quite suddenly at the end of yesterday's lesson. This was because I had run out of time. Miss O'Malley told me I was making excellent progress and she wished she did not have to stop me. I do not know how she can say I am making progress as I still have not said one word to her. In fact, she spent the whole of the last lesson sitting at her desk whistling. She is the first woman I have ever met who whistles. She whistles very well, though.

Although she is nice, I do not really want to speak to her much. I just know that I would say the word "hands" at a really stupid moment and make her feel bad about herself. This is not something I want to do.

Today we sat down again and she gave me a glass of squash and a custard cream.

Custard Creams

I love custard creams.

In fact, they are my absolute number one favourite biscuit.[7] In between the two pieces of biscuit, the custard just seems so *cosy*. It shows just enough of itself to let you know what you are getting but it does not go the whole hog. I wish more people would think like a custard cream when it comes to their clothes. They should keep a little bit of themselves back instead of flashing their custard everywhere.

As I munched on my biscuit and sipped the violently strong squash,[8] she told me I must stop thinking of Dealing With Feelings as being lessons. I must call them "sessions" instead. She must have read my stuff from last week. I mean, it is not like I have ever called it a lesson to her face.

"The word 'lessons' implies I'm teaching you something here," she said, in her wispy sort of voice. "I'm not. We're here together to explore what makes you tick and for us to investigate how we can move on from everything that's happened."

I shrugged.

"What you need to do, Michael, is to step out of the box.

---

7 Followed by: 2) Rich tea (plain but dependable) 3) Pink wafers (light and fun without being *too* sweet or silly) and 4) Plain digestives (solid, delicious and almost healthy).

8 She measured it out with her finger again but today I am one step ahead of her. I have brought a bottle of water to the lesson – sorry, *session* – and will discreetly dilute the squash as I go along, without her knowing.

Take a look at yourself. This is not a classroom. It's more a *discovery suite*."

Explore? Investigate? Discovery? She makes it sound like we are hunting for shrunken heads in the Amazon.

I am not interested in taking a look at myself (I look a bit weird) or stepping out of the box. Boxes are good. They are comfortable and contained and they protect you from everything outside.[9]

When I did not reply, she waved a giant hand at the laptop, which was waiting on the desk. I smiled politely, sat down and began to type.

The Changing Room
Just Before The First Disaster

So I had just been thrown out of the swimming session. When I got into the changing rooms, Paul was sprawled out on a bench, looking really pleased with himself. "Hey, you're finished early," he said, grinning.

"What were you doing out there?" I said, shoving my bag down violently.

---

9 I once spent three hours in a big furniture box when I was four. I really enjoyed myself in there . . . until my idiot brother broke wind into it with terrifying violence, then slammed the lid shut, trapping me inside.

Paul rubbed his hands together. "Checking out Miss King, of course. Same as you."

"I was *training*, you massive whale," I snarled.

Paul looked hurt. He has a face like a giant baby. "Hey. That's not fair. I was born this way. Anyway, don't give me that training rubbish. You hate swimming. You moan about it every day."

He had me there. I felt myself getting red. "Yeah. Well. At least I was *trying* to *pretend* to swim. How can I get better if I do not take tips from the best? You were just staring at her like you were at an aquarium."

Paul went all misty-eyed. "And what a view it was. I was poking around the garage last night and found all of my dad's old scuba stuff. Soon as I saw that mask I thought. . ."

"You thought you would use it to perv on Lucy King. You are a menace to society." I pulled open my bag and took a puff on my inhaler. "She called us pathetic."

Paul pulled off his shorts. I quickly turned away. There are certain things on Earth that I do not *ever* want to see. This definitely includes whatever it is that lurks inside Paul Beary's shorts.

"Whoa whoa whoa! She must've called *you* pathetic. She said nothing to me."

"Lucy would not call me pathetic. I know she would not."

Paul flicked me with his wet towel. "Mike. She doesn't even know who you are."

I jumped to my feet, just managing to keep my eyes away from him. "Rubbish. She smiled at me once."

"No, Mike," sighed Paul. "She *laughed* at you once. I was there. We've been through this before. There's a difference."

I shook my head. "Smiled."

Paul took a deep breath. "Mike. It was definitely a laugh."

"How do *you* know?"

"A duck had just crapped on your head. She laughed so hard I thought she was going to throw up."

"Not true," I muttered. "Not true."

There was silence for a moment, then Paul said, "Anyway, hurry up. I haven't had any breakfast yet and there were only two packs of fruit pastilles left in the vending machine when I came in."

I know for a fact that Paul Beary sometimes eats fruit pastilles for breakfast because "they've got fruit in so they must be good for me". He once told me that they make his breath smell fresher than toothpaste so he does not need to brush his teeth either. He said that this is like "pulling two girls with one chat-up line". I do not think he has ever "pulled" one girl, let alone two.

The only time I eat anything sweet for breakfast is on Sundays, birthdays and during school holidays. I used to eat Coco Pops, before everything happened. I see them as a relaxed, weekend sort of cereal. They are almost like party food but at breakfast time.

From Monday to Friday during the summer I eat cornflakes and two slices of toast (butter, no jam). In the winter it is always porridge. These seem to be more suitable breakfast choices for weekdays. I would feel very wrong wearing a school tie and eating a chocolatey or sugary breakfast cereal. The thought of it makes me a little queasy. The night after Paul first told me about his fruit pastille breakfast, I had a nightmare about opening my cornflakes and there being only fruit pastilles inside. This caused a massive asthma attack.

Anyway, it is a shame I will never eat Coco Pops again. I suppose that, soon enough, I will have to explain why.

Getting Changed

I have already mentioned that I do not like to be watched. However, this should be extended. I DO NOT LIKE TO BE LOOKED AT WHATSOEVER. I have what you might call an unusual body. This is composed of: big feet, skinny arms, a pigeon chest, a pot belly and a massive head that waggles when I walk. My brother says I look like a string puppet. He is an idiot.

As long as I can remember I have hated to be looked at. Still, my mum has forced me to do a sport like swimming, for which I have to wear only a pair of trunks. Usually I wrap myself in a towel or a dressing gown until I am just about to dive in.

One of the worst times was in Year 7. I woke up one day and found to my horror that I had grown an extra, well, *nipple* on my chest.

Yes, an extra nipple.

This made me very self-conscious. I pretended to be ill so that I could avoid swimming and refused to get changed for PE at school. I could not tell anyone and *definitely* could not go to the school nurse. I did not even dare to touch it in case it *pulsated* or something.

Then, after four days of fear and terror, it fell off in the bath. It turned out that it was just a baked bean that my idiot brother had superglued to my skin whilst I was asleep.

Anyway, as a result, I do not like getting changed near other people. Just being at the swimming pool is bad enough. So, despite Paul Beary laughing at me and saying I looked like an old woman, I wrapped my towel around my chest like a dress and got out of my trunks and into my clothes as quickly as possible.

Bear Hug From Miss O'Malley

Miss O'Malley has just patted me on the shoulder. Her hand was so heavy it was like having an eagle land on me. She told me the time was up. Apart from her whistling, I had forgotten she was there.

"OK, Michael," she said, "time to stop."

Without thinking, I said, "Please can I finish writing this bit?"

I guess I felt like I had more to say.

Do you know what she did? Out of nowhere she hugged me tight. I mean really tight. I thought she was going to snap a rib. Then she started spraying words out like a machine gun. "Oh well done. Well done, Michael. Finally he speaks to me. At last. At last. Dear Lord, I thought he was a mute. So brave. So very very brave. Of course you can finish. Stay as long as you like and I'll let your teachers know what a brave lad you are."

I did not have a clue what she was on about. I certainly did not *feel* brave. All I did was ask her for more time. I smiled a little. Then we both kind of looked at each other in silence. It was a bit awkward, really. After what seemed like ages, I turned back to the laptop and carried on typing. She went back to whistling at her desk. As soon as I finish this next bit of the story, I am getting out of here.

Outside the Leisure Centre

I spent at least twenty-five minutes by the vending machines with Paul. I always buy the same thing after training. A straightforward milk chocolate bar. There is no messing about with stuff you do not need inside it – just chocolate and nothing else. Money in. Press D3. Reach down. Eat. Same every week.

Paul, however, does not go to the vending machine with a plan. He puts his money in, *then* starts to think about what he might buy. The whole time, he commentates on the choices on offer. This is stupid as it wastes time and is seriously annoying for the people behind him. Soon a queue developed. A few of them were checking their watches and muttering to themselves as he started saying things like, "No, not wine gums, I've had them three times this week, never liked Murray Mints, not a *big* fan of nuts, water is just out of the question. No fruit pastilles left, I knew I should have got them before I came in. Got to strike while the iron's hot." When I told him about the people behind, he started getting red-faced, punching buttons angrily and at random.

Outside, he was moaning, as usual. "Why did you start rushing me? I didn't want bacon-flavoured crisps *and* fruit gums."

"That's as close to a balanced breakfast as you get," I said, sarcastically.

Paul sniffed. "Yeah, I suppose it is. Meat and fruit. Hey. Isn't that your brother?"

My heart sank. Paul was right. Leaning against the side of his car (which was parked in the disabled space even though he is not disabled) was my older brother Ste.

"D'you reckon he'll give us a lift?" Paul said, spraying me with bacon-crisp crumbs.

I snorted. "Paul. Even if you had the crisp crumbs jet-washed off you and you were shrink-wrapped inside a giant plastic bag, he would not let you inside that car. It means more to him than life itself."

This is absolutely true. One time Ste was at our house with one of his many girlfriends. She cut her finger on a tin of beans and was bleeding really badly, and I mean *gushing* all over the place. She started freaking out and told him that he *had* to get her to hospital straight away. So do you know what he did? He drove her to the hospital but made her hold her hand out of the window the whole way there so no blood got on to the seats. Then he dumped her for "almost staining his car".

"Hey hey hey, losers!" called my brother, removing his sunglasses.

"Oh brilliant. He has seen us," I groaned.

Reasons why I hate my brother:

1. He has a goatee beard. I hate beards, especially ones that look like slugs clinging to people's lips. This has nothing to do with the fact that he can grow a beard and I cannot.
2. Whenever he gets a spot, he uses ladies' make-up to cover it. He thinks no one can notice it but sometimes, when you get up close, you can see all these orangey-pink crusty bits on his face.[10]
3. Four years ago, he and his friends blew cigar smoke into

---

10 Paul suffers from a similar problem after they serve apple pie and custard at the school canteen.

my hamster's cage when my parents were out. This was "hilarious". However, I am certain that this caused Humphrey to develop breathing problems. After that fateful day, the poor little thing would wheeze like an old man after just a few minutes in his spinning wheel.[11]

4. He owns a car. Not just any car, either. A VW Golf GTi with 1.6 litre engine, alloy wheels, leather interior, personalized plates (C00L S13 – with illegal screws on either side of the 1 to make it look like a T), a five-hundred-pound stereo system with bass bins that could burst your eardrums, a sticker in the back which reads "the passion wagon" and a fluffy Eeyore toy hanging from the rear-view mirror "for the ladies". I would estimate that ninety per cent of his time is spent cruising around in his car, honking his horn at girls. He once told me that, if I were on fire and there was a smear of grease on his windscreen, he would not even consider using the windscreen washers on his car to extinguish me. The car was paid for after Ste broke his leg playing football a few years ago, then claimed that he had tripped on a dodgy paving slab. He sued the council for over six thousand pounds. The rest he paid for through the protection fee he charged me throughout Years 7

---

11 When Humphrey died two years later, Mum said it was from old age. To this day, however, I remain positive that it was lung disease. May he rest in peace.

and 8, and money he wangled out of Mum and Dad. Somehow, he still has enough money that he is planning to go to Australia for a year after his A levels.

5. Girls in our school seem to find him good-looking. I have lost track of how many times I have been stopped in the corridors by giggling girls and asked stupid things like, "Are you Sexy Ste in the sixth form's brother?" One girl asked me if I had any holiday snaps of him in his swimming shorts and offered me ten quid for one. When I asked her why she thought I would carry one round with me, she stamped on my foot and called me "an ugly little hobbit".
6. When I was five, I was on a donkey ride at the beach. Ste ran up behind the donkey and whacked it on the bum. The donkey went crazy, sprinting off across the sand before skidding to a halt and hurling me over a fence. I still have a scar under my chin and a mortal fear of donkeys.

"Nice wheels, Ste," said Paul, stroking the front of the car.

Ste slapped his hand off. "Hey hey hey, half-ton man. Don't touch what you can't afford. Keep your sticky fingers off the passion wagon."

Ste is always saying things like "hey hey hey", and "don't touch what you can't afford". Sometimes he even calls himself "The Stevenator". As I think I have mentioned before, he is an idiot.

"What are you doing here?" I sighed.

"The Stevenator is here to pick you boys up. Thought you might want a lift."

"Really?" said Paul, a bit too eagerly.

Ste grinned widely. "Of course not. The only reason I'd let you two lame-o's in the back of The Beast is if you were strapped up to two hot ladies with massive . . . *hey hey hey*, gorgeous!"

I followed Ste's eyes, which were suddenly looking over my shoulder. Skipping down the steps outside the leisure centre, her hair all tousled from the pool and a big smile plastered across her face, came Lovely Lucy King.

What was she doing?

Ste gave her this soppy little wave and then growled under his breath. "Get out of here, you pair of winnets. You're obstructing the mysterious forces of human attraction."

I struggled for breath. "What are you. . ."

He was not. . . She *was not*. . .

My voice trailed off as I realized he was completely ignoring me. Lucy bounded over to him and do you know what he did?

He kissed her right on the lips. The lips. *In public*.

My ribs turned to ice and froze my heart. Paul's mouth was open and he was quite brazenly drooling all over his chin.

After about five seconds (way longer than was necessary), I gave a loud cough. The two lovebirds slowly turned round and stared at me. Ste narrowed his eyes like some kind of angry reptile. Lucy looked really puzzled by my presence.

My face started to burn and I felt a tickle at the back of my throat. "How . . . long . . . have. . ."

Ste gave a smile that would easily have won him the world's smuggest man contest. "Well, me and the lovely Lucy hooked up last week, and when she told me her name, I thought she must spell it L-U-C-K-Y cos that was the luckiest day of my life."

At that moment I genuinely could have puked. If I had not been scared of getting killed for splashing Ste's car, I would have done, too. And do you know what Lucy did when she heard this sickening rubbish? She wrinkled up her nose, put her arm round Ste's waist and made the kind of noise most people only make when they see a deformed kitten.

Ste ruffled my hair. "And these little champs are my brother Mikey and his mate Paul."[12]

Lucy pursed her lips like she had just had to swallow down some stomach bile. "Oh yes. I know these two."

I made a pathetic whimpering sound.

Ste's eyes flicked towards the front of the leisure centre. "Right then, guys. Love to stay but we're going to get off. Lucy's trying on new swimming costumes this afternoon and

---

12 Whenever Ste is trying to impress a girl, he pretends to like me and puts on this whole caring big brother act. One time – and this is a fact – he squashed me into my old pushchair and pushed me round the park all day while he chatted up girls because, apparently, "women love babies". I was ten years old.

she needs an honest opinion on what fits."

Lucy playfully slapped him on the arm. I wished she had smacked him in the face. As he manoeuvred her into the car, do you know what he did? He touched her.

On the bum.

The swine.

I could have cried, and not just because it reminded me of when he slapped the donkey on the backside.

As he closed the door behind her, he looked up to the front of the leisure centre again. His face suddenly went pale and he quickly hopped into his car and roared off, leaving a cloud of aftershave and exhaust fumes behind him.

I turned around and looked up to where Ste had been staring. Dave King was standing, hands on hips, glaring at my brother's car as it disappeared through the gates. No wonder Ste had rushed off. It was the kind of glare that could maim someone.

Looking back now, I guess I quite liked that look on Dave's face. It made me feel really relieved. Maybe he would do something. If anyone could keep my brother's greasy mitts off Lucy, it was him.

Dealing With Feelings Session 4

I arrived at Miss O'Malley's room five minutes late today. This got me so flustered that I needed three puffs on my inhaler. As

I have already mentioned, I do not like to be late. One time I was late for a bus. It is not an interesting story but I hated watching it sail away along the road without me so much that it has stuck with me ever since. It messed up my plans for the whole afternoon. I like things to be organized. I had to catch the next bus instead. This meant that one of the things on my to-do list for that day (buy hand lotion for my eczema) was not done. The next day my hands were so flaky they looked like a pair of overcooked sausage rolls. This is proof that being late is a bad thing.

Today, however, it was not my fault that I was late. When I was on my way to the session, I saw Lucy King standing in the middle of the playground. I had not seen her at school for a few weeks. Today must be her first day back after everything that happened. Her black eye looked healed but I still guessed she did not want to see me. This meant I had to take a detour right the way around the outside of the upper school building just to avoid her. Then, just when I thought I was safe, I saw Miss Skinner, the goss-eyed art teacher, coming the other way. I do not think she saw me (you never can tell with her wonky eyes) but I had to hide in an empty classroom until she had gone past. I am not ready to speak to her yet either.

When I arrived, I knocked but there was no answer. I looked inside. Miss O'Malley was not here. I took the opportunity to look around the room a bit. These are some of the things in here:

1. Six posters on the wall. Topics in alphabetical order: alcohol, bullying, cigarettes, germs, hand-washing and nits.
2. A neat desk containing two first-aid kits, a box of rubber bands and a framed photo of a horse. I shuddered when I saw this. Ever since the donkey incident I have hated all hooved animals.
3. A soft bench with a brown blanket on it. The blanket has several large, crusty stains on it. I do not want to know what they are but this is where kids lie down when they are not feeling well.
4. Two large bottles of squash and a biscuit barrel.
5. A box of latex gloves. Size: XXXL (I knew it!).

I decided to try on one of the gloves. It was easily one and a half times the size of a normal glove. I could make a fist and squeeze my whole hand into just the thumb hole. I slipped it off and put it back in the box, then realized this was not hygienic and put it in my pocket instead. At this point I made a mental note that, if I ever need to dress as a chicken, I will paint the fingers red and wear it on my head as it will definitely stretch around my skull. I then spent a good few seconds wondering why I would ever need to dress as a chicken.

On the desk, I also found the laptop, which was on. My file was open so she had definitely been reading my stuff again (surprisingly, I do not think that this bothers me at all).

Next to the laptop was half a pack of biscuits. Unfortunately they were Bourbon creams. I do not like these biscuits for two reasons: A) they remind me of my brother; B) they are nowhere near as good as custard creams (my absolute favourites) even though they are supposed to be a jazzier version. Still, they are (very slightly) better than nothing, and Miss O'Malley knows nothing about how much I dislike them. She is at least trying to be kind. Therefore I will force one or two down just to show my gratitude.

There was a note that read, "Dear Michael. Please carry on with your writing. Sorry I can't be there. I have had to go and meet someone. It is a shame as I felt we were making progress but this person I am meeting could be good for you. I'll tell you about it later. I hope I can get him to visit."

When I read about this mystery person I shuddered. I do not like surprises. I never liked surprises anyway but the reason I *really* do not like them now will become clear very soon. Out of everything that happened to me, the surprises were the worst part of all.

Why I Really Do Not Like Surprises

After my brother had driven off, Paul and I left the leisure centre. Usually on a Saturday I would go into town after training and put some of my pocket money into my bank account. I feel that it is never too early to think about the future. However, until now I have never told anyone that I am a regular saver.[13] As I did not want to have to either explain to Paul where I was going or make up a lie, I decided to just go straight home instead. I could always leave the money in my piggy bank until the following Saturday.

I did not realize it at the time, but this decision would mean that I arrived home several hours earlier than expected.

This was to lead to devastating consequences.

When we turned the corner into my road, Paul was jumping up and down like a Labrador puppy. "Can you believe your brother's probably snogging Lucy King right at this moment?"

"No," I said, grinding my teeth together. I had thought of nothing else since we left the leisure centre. It was making me feel quite sick.

"You know, me and your Ste have got a lot in common," he said.

"Like what?" I groaned.

I was genuinely expecting him to reveal that Ste loved bacon-flavoured crisps and stealing scuba equipment to spy on young athletes too.

Paul sniffed. "We're both a hit with the ladies."

---

13 Paul would call me a geek. My brother would try to steal my bank details. Then call me a geek.

I stopped in the middle of the road. "Ladies? What are you talking about? Have you even met a lady without harassing her?"

Paul stuck his bottom lip out like a sulky three-year-old. "I've had a girlfriend, I'll have you know. She was. . ."

"French, I know," I said. "She was deeply impressed by the fact that your uncle invented the mobile home."

"Caravan," scowled Paul.

We walked on in silence right to the end of my street, then he suddenly said, "Hey! Can I look at that book up in your bedroom?"

That book is called *My Body is Changing.* It is by a silly person called Floella Rampazzo. It is one of those awful books about growing up that you get. My mum bought it for me and left it on my bedside table last year. It is full of chapters with titles like "Hair Today, More Tomorrow", "Low Down on Lice", and "B.O. – It's the Pits". Paul loves it because it is full of cartoon pictures of naked people. He is a very sad boy.

When we got to my front door, I noticed that the curtains were shut.

I should have turned around then. I really should have done. It should have been obvious that something was wrong. I mean, who has their curtains closed in the middle of the day? Murderers? Gangsters? Members of sinister cults?

The truth, it turned out, was far worse.

The Absolute Worst Moment of My Entire Life (Until Then, Anyway)

A simple plan of my house: the front door opens into the hallway, which has three doors off it. One is at the end of the hall. It goes into the dining room. The one on the left goes into the little toilet under the stairs. This is my favourite of the two toilets in the house as Ste does not use it. This means there are no pots of hair gel by the sink, no gloopy blotches of the ladies' make-up he uses to hide his spots on the carpet, and no goatee trimmings blocking the plughole. On the right-hand side of the hall there is a door into the front room, which is always, always open.

On this day, the door was closed.

This was another sign that not everything was hunky-dory. If my brain had not been full of the thought of Ste snogging Lucy King, I would have realized that something was seriously wrong.

"Can I go and look at the book now?" said Paul, already kicking off his shoes and sprinting upstairs three at a time.[14]

---

14 I do not like to keep on about Paul's weight but last month he was given an exercise plan by his doctor. He never did any of it. I think the doctor should have just hidden a load of slightly rude cartoon pictures at the top of a block of flats. Paul would have run up thirty flights of stairs every day without question.

I looked at the closed door of the lounge. From inside I could hear muffled voices. Wearing a puzzled frown, I opened the door.

I was not prepared for what I saw.

My mum and dad were in the front room. Mum was sitting down. Dad was standing up, pouring her a cup of tea from a teapot.

They were both nude.

Nude.

Naked. Unclothed. Without even a stitch. Everything on show. All pink and plump and bare like two Christmas turkeys. Dangly bits dangling. Wobbly bits wobbling. Tufts of hair sprouting up everywhere. Lumps, bumps and saggy rumps all quivering as the two of them stared back at me, open-mouthed. Dad's pot belly and the teapot were thankfully blocking out my view of Mum's you-know-whats.

It was disgusting. Foul. Weird. Indescribably horrible. I had never seen them undressed before. They looked like two badly shaved chimpanzees. The sight of their underwear on the washing line is enough to make me queasy. This was preposterous. I thought my head would explode.

There was a splashing sound.

The tea was overflowing Mum's cup. Dad let out a yelp and jumped backwards with everything bouncing everywhere as the scalding tea poured on to his foot. I noticed at this point that he was wearing socks. This struck me as very bizarre, even when you consider everything else that was going on.

"Michael, I can explain," said Mum, standing up.

I can assure you that this was not what I wanted to see. It completely tipped me over the edge. I had not expected her to move or talk and I certainly did not want to see what was staring me in the face at that moment in time. I was kind of hoping they were not really my mum and dad, just a pair of wax statues who had not been given their clothes yet.

At this point everything in my memory blurs together. I remember her taking a step towards me. My mouth going dry. Me covering my eyes. A scream trying to escape my lips. Pelting it upstairs. Mum's footsteps behind me. Staggering through my bedroom door, wheezing. Paul ogling the pictures in my growing-up book. Collapsing flat out on the floor.

Everything going black.

Miss O'Malley Returns

A couple of minutes ago, Miss O'Malley came back in but I did not acknowledge her straight away. I was halfway through writing so I did not want to stop. It seemed important to finish writing about what had happened.

After hitting the last full stop in that section, I finally turned around. Miss O'Malley looked excited. She told me I was very lucky; tomorrow I would be having a visitor to the session. I asked her who it was and she just whistled in a "wouldn't you like to know but I'm not going to tell you because it's a big surprise and it would totally spoil it if I told you now so you're just going to have to wait, aren't you" kind of way.

I did not like this one bit. For a start, I did not trust the way she whistled at me. My dad once told me never to trust a plumber who whistles when you ask him how much a job is going to cost. I know that Miss O'Malley is not a plumber (I think her hands would be far too big to fiddle with pipes anyway) but I think the point is that people can whistle when they are being dishonest. *That* was definitely a dishonest whistle.

I kind of shuddered when she whistled at me so she backed off and left me alone and began pretending to tidy her shelves. This is about all I can handle for one day.

Dealing With Feelings Session 5

Today was not a good start to the session. When I arrived in the room, Miss O'Malley was sitting next to a man who I had never seen before. The best way to describe him would be long. He had a long thin body, a long nose, a long grey ponytail that hung right the way down his back and long yellow teeth. He was wearing skinny jeans that clung to his long, scrawny legs, huge clumpy basketball trainers and a baseball cap. Honestly. *A baseball cap.* He must have been pushing fifty years old.

"Yo, dude," he said as I came in (I swear on my life – *dude*). "How's it hanging?"

I frowned a bit at Miss O'Malley, who tried to reassure me with a huge smile. "Michael, I'd like you to meet Chas. You remember the person I went to meet the other day? Well, Chas was that person. He's a lecturer from the university. I told you we'd be having a visitor."

Chas (I am assuming his real name is Charles) made a gun shape with two fingers and clicked his tongue. This drew his lips back over his pointy teeth, giving him the appearance of some kind of starved guinea pig.

"Good grief," I said.

"Radical," Chas said.[15]

"Glass of squash, anyone?" Miss O'Malley said.

"Check," said Chas. As Miss O'Malley busied herself at the far side of the room, Chas tapped the laptop, which was on. "So, man. Pretty heavy stuff going on at home, eh?"

I did not like this. Not in the slightest bit. He had read my writing. This was not good. It bothered me ten million times more than when Miss O'Malley had read it.

Miss O'Malley must have noticed my face drop. "Oh, Michael, I am sorry I didn't tell you before. I rang your mum.

---

15 I might not be up to date with the latest slang, but even I know that nobody has used the word "radical" in this way since about 1986.

She gave Chas permission to, you know, have a look at your thoughts. Did she not ask you?"

Well that is just typical of my mum. Not only has she ruined my thoughts for ever, but now she owns the rights to them as well. All right, so I *may* have been living in a tent in the back garden and refusing to speak to her for over a week now but that is not the point. She could have written me a letter to ask my permission, or even used a messenger pigeon. "No," I said stiffly, "strangely enough she did not."

Chas rubbed his hands together. "So, the beautiful Miss O'Malley tells me you don't speak much since everything that's gone on, eh?"

I shrugged. In the background, I could hear Miss O'Malley chuckling with delight at being called beautiful.

"That's cool, man. That's totally cool. I can dig where you're coming from. You know, I like a man of few words. Now, let me get down to it. I am a psychologist."

A shrink. Wonderful – Miss O'Malley must have told him that I am mental.

Chas seemed to notice my alarm. "Don't worry about it, M-Dog. I ain't gonna do anything bad. I specialize in kids with issues, you know? Things not going right at home, bullying, eating disorders, bed-wetting, that sort of thing."

I felt my eyebrows rise up. Chas did not seem to notice. He sniffed and spun his baseball cap round so it was back to front. *Back to front.* I will just repeat here that he is fifty years old.

"So, Miss O'M rocks up to me at the uni yesterday and gives me the beef on all your problems."

I shot an angry glance at Miss O'Malley but she was suddenly and very intently studying the nutritional information on the side of the squash bottle.

"Anyway, so I sweet-talked your head teacher to find out more about your case. And guess what, big guy? I found out that you are a kid I'd love to meet."

Unbelievable. They must have told him everything. Surely there are laws about this. Seemingly not, though. I mean, why *would* there be a law to stop strange-looking men from spying on my personal thoughts? Mum might as well have just given him permission to take my brain out and have a good old poke around.

"So, we all agreed that you should maybe spend a bit of time with me down at the uni, you know? Couple of afternoons out of school, chat with me and my students, check out some hot older babes, eh?"

He leered at me and punched me lightly in the arm. I winced.

"That's great," he smiled, revealing his fangs again. As he stood up to leave he clicked his fingers at Miss O'Malley. "I'll get my peeps to sort the deets this very afternoon and I'll see you tomorrow, little buddy. Hey, and Mikey. Keep writing it down, babe. Keep writing it down."

Babe? I could not believe this was happening.

When he left, Miss O'Malley had a big warm grin on her face. "What do you think of Chas, then?"

"He is an idiot," I said.

This time when I spoke, she did not give me a hug or tell me I was brave like last time. Instead, she slammed a glass of squash down on the desk so hard I thought it would smash, then started angrily filing something into a folder at the back of the room.

I guess she likes him.

It took me a while before I felt like writing.

The Absolute Worst Moment of My Entire Life Part II

When I left off last time, I had just hit the ground. I have no idea how long I was unconscious for. The next thing I knew, I felt sick and there were three pink blobs swirling above me. Slowly, the blobs stopped moving, became clearer and turned into the staring faces of Mum, Dad and Paul Beary.

Paul Beary!

I sat up like a shot, almost headbutting all three of them. Thankfully, Mum and Dad were both wearing bathrobes. "He did not see you, did he? Tell me he did not see you."

Mum cleared her throat. Dad scratched his bald patch.

Paul licked his lips and raised one eyebrow. "I tried not to look, Mike, but she just ran in after you. I wasn't expecting her to be in the nu. . ."

"OUT!" I growled, scrambling to my feet and grabbing him by his collar. "Get out now. And tell no one."

"All right, all right! Jeez, someone's tired," said Paul, shaking me off and walking to the door. He turned to my mum with a huge smile. "Thanks for your hospitality, Mrs Swarbrick. I'll be sure to call again."

I picked up the copy of *My Body is Changing* that Paul had left on the floor and hurled it at him as hard as I could. It just missed his head as he ducked out through the door.

When his footsteps had thudded down the stairs and the front door had clicked shut, Mum turned to me. Her mouth was turned down like she was sucking on a nettle. "Michael, I can explain. We weren't expecting you back so soon. Normally you're back much later. I guess we just forgot."

"Forgot what?" I snapped, sitting on my bed. "Your pants?"

Mum rolled her eyes. "Now you're being immature."

"Immature?" I felt my breathing getting quicker. "But I have just seen your moomies."

"My what?"

I waved my hand up and down at her body.

"Oh for heaven's sake, Michael. What did you see? My skin? My body? They aren't dirty words, Michael." She ran her hand through her hair. "How did I bring up such an uptight child?"

I clenched my fists and looked at the wall. This whole thing was far too much for me to deal with. I had never even seen them in their swimming costumes before, let alone *naked*.[16]

Dad coughed. "Well, son. You know your mother wanted to . . . well, you know it was her idea to . . . you see, the thing is. . ."

Mum tutted. "Oh stop it, Roy. Don't blame me for everything. Look, Michael. Your father and I are naturists."

My breathing was getting really shallow now. "Naturists? You mean you go out in the countryside like that? You are disgusting. What about the sheep? You will scare them to death."

"No, Michael," groaned Mum, "naturists. Nudists. People who prefer to be as nature intended. We just want to be free, Michael. *Free* from the handcuffs of society. *Free* from the prisons of our clothes. *Free* as the birds in the sky and the dolphins in the sea. Out in the fresh air, sun on our skin, wind blowing through our. . ."

"All right, all right," I said, by now struggling for my breath. "What were you doing in the front room, then? I have to sit on that chair, you know."

Mum looked at Dad, who seemed fascinated by a piece of fluff on the sleeve of his dressing gown. "We're . . . erm, practising."

"Practising?" I said, my chest getting tighter and tighter. "Practising for what?"

---

16 Despite Mum having forced me to swim since I was four and a half, she cannot swim herself.

Dad winced. "Going . . . outside."

"Outside?" I gasped, struggling for breath. I grabbed my inhaler and took two deep puffs on it. "Tell . . . me . . . you are . . . joking."

"No, Michael," said Mum. "This is really important to your father and me."

"Well," said Dad, "it's more important to your mother."

Mum shot him a dirty look. "Not this again, Roy. You always put everything on me. More than eight years of building up to it, and you still can't take your socks off in the house."

I was seriously unable to breathe now. "Eight . . . years?! You have been . . . walking . . . round . . . in the . . . nude . . . for eight years . . . in my house? Dis . . . gusting." I suddenly realized something. "Hang on a second . . . this is . . . why you . . . never watch me train . . . on a Saturday. This . . . is . . . your . . . ewww . . . nudey time!"

I spat the last words out like two mouthfuls of rotten tangerine.

"Darling, that's not fair," said Mum.

"Fair," I gulped. "Fair? The image of your naked bodies . . . is burned into my retinas. . . I am afraid . . . to blink in case . . . I see you again. I wish I could . . . pull out my eyes."

This last sentence was as much as I could manage. It felt like a cold hand was gripping my lungs and squeezing out the air. I staggered across the room and fell to the floor, clutching my throat.

"Michael, are you OK?" said Mum.

"Where's your bag, son?" said Dad.

I waved my hands at the bedside table, sweat pouring off my forehead. My breath sounded like a piece of wood being sawed in half.

Mum grabbed the brown paper bag that I keep for asthma attacks off my bedside table. She held it to my mouth, gently rubbing my back as I breathed in and out of it.

"That's it, son. Nice and steady," said Dad, as my breath slowly calmed down.

Mum rubbed my back in circles. "I'm so sorry, Michael. I'm so, so sorry. We shouldn't have shocked you like that. The thing is, now it's out in the open I feel like a great weight has been lifted. Finally we don't need to creep around. You know about us, so why should we hide it any more? You know, I think you'll get used to it."

I grabbed the paper bag off her, held it to my mouth and continued breathing in and out.

Chatting With Chas

Session 1 Transcript[17]

People Present

17 As recorded, typed up and emailed to me by the students who were hiding behind a one-way mirror in the room. All footnotes are mine.

Swarbrick, Michael - subject (hereafter "MS")
Swaffham-Bunstable, Professor Charles Algenon (hereafter "Chas"[18])

Location

University of Preston (UP), Psychology Dept., Observation Studio 2

Context Notes

MS is a fourteen-year-old boy with serious issues of self-image, originating from his (subjectively) unusual appearance.[19] As a result, he has a tendency to concentrate excessively on the physical imperfections of others. E.g., in his feelings journal, he speculates frequently about the size of his counsellor's hands.

The subject appears to have unresolved feelings of lust for Lucy King - a talented local swimmer - and displays a range of obsessive tendencies. These have manifested themselves through:

- Michael's uncontrolled jealousy over Ms King's

---

18 I knew it – a posh name. The transcript does not mention that he was wearing a T-shirt that said "Rave Till the Grave" on the front in bright pink letters.
19 I looked this up in the dictionary. It means that they think I look weird.

romantic involvement with his brother, Steven.

- what police describe as Michael "stalking" Ms King.[20]

He has recently discovered that his parents are nudists - a revelation for which he was hopelessly unprepared because of his crippling emotional immaturity[21] and obsession with order and control. This has led to various incidents involving the police, the result of which is his attendance at regular counselling sessions with his school nurse. Despite this, he is still unable to communicate his problems or indeed find a solution to them.

Transcript

Chas: Yo, Mikey.

MS: (. . .)

Chas: How's it hanging?

MS: (. . .) [*Shrugs shoulders and stares at the one-way mirror.*]

[Eight-second pause.]

Chas: I thought that we could call these sessions

---

20 I did not stalk her. I just made sure that I knew a lot about her. There is a huge difference.

21 I looked this up too. They think I am a big baby.

Chatting With Chas. How do you feel about that?

MS: (. . .) [*Looks briefly at Chas, then continues to stare at the one-way mirror.*]

Chas: So, Mikey. What's going on with you at the moment? Still sleeping in the tent?

[Fifteen-second pause. MS continues to stare at the one-way mirror.]

Chas: Anything you want to talk about?

[Thirty-five-second pause. MS continues to stare at the one-way mirror.]

MS: Are there people on the other side of that mirror?

Chas: Yes, buddy. There are.

MS: What are they doing?

Chas: They're just checking out what's going down.

MS: Why?

Chas: You're an interesting kid.

MS: No, I am not.

Chas: Why do you think that?

[Four-minute pause.]

MS: Please may I go home now?

Chas: Yeah, buddy. You go for it. Great talking to you. Interesting.

MS: I might call it something else. [*MS disconnects his microphone and exits the room.*]

Chas: [*After MS has exited, speaking towards the students behind the one-way mirror.*] See, guys. That's how you do it. Get down to their level and they'll let you in. He doesn't like to be looked at.[22] Notice that. You mightn't think he said much, but where did he want to go? Home. The nest. The cocoon. The only place he feels safe. But read the notes, people. This kid is, and I use my own term here, seriously messed up.[23] Home's where his problems are. Him saying that that's where he's going tells us a lot. What does it tell us? He wants to get to the root of his issues. Next time he'll sing like a canary.

[Ten-second pause.]

Chas: OK, who's coming to the pub?

[Seven-second pause.]

Chas: What? All of you are busy? Oh. OK. Next time.

[End of transcript]

22 Especially not by a bunch of faceless students hiding behind a mirror.

23 This coming from *him*! Un-be-lievable.

Dealing With Feelings Session 6

After Chatting With Chas, the university paid for a taxi to take me back to school. Then I came straight here to Miss O'Malley's room. When I sat down, she asked me how my first session with Chas went. I said that it was rubbish and asked her if I had to go again.

Miss O'Malley whistled long and hard, then said, "Well, isn't that a fine attitude to have. You might as well just give up on all your hard work if that's how you feel."

She cracked her huge knuckles.[24] Then she started noisily sorting out the little grey cardboard vomit trays and muttering under her breath. I guessed it would be for the best if I turned on the laptop.

Before I started writing, I quickly checked my emails. The transcript of the meeting with Chas had already been forwarded to me. Reading it back, I suppose I may not have been too cooperative with Chas but I do not think I could have helped it. He is a seriously strange person.

The Coco Pops Incident

The morning after The Absolute Worst Moment of My Entire

---

24 The crack was so loud I thought for a moment that she'd shot me.

Life (Parts I and II), I was minding my own business, sitting down in the dining room with a bowl of Coco Pops in front of me (it was a Sunday, after all, so it felt perfectly natural to be eating a sugary breakfast), reading the comics from inside the paper. Without warning, Mum and Dad walked in.

They were nude.

"What are you doing?" I yelled, pulling the comic up in front of my eyes.

"Oh, don't be ridiculous, Michael," said Mum, sitting down right next to me. "The secret's out now. No point in hiding it. In fact, I feel liberated. Free. We aren't living a lie now and it's great. You walking in on us was the best thing that's ever happened. No more excuses from your father that he's frightened of being caught by you."

Dad rubbed his hands up and down his arms. "It *is* a bit chilly, though. You don't mind if I go upstairs and put on a dressing gown, do you?"

Mum tutted. "Yes, I do mind. It's important you acclimatize. How else will you adapt to the great outdoors?"

"You are really going to do it," I said. "You are really going to go out there and show the world your—"

"Yes, Michael, we are," said Mum. "Now get over your prudish silliness and put that comic down. You can't eat your breakfast like that."

I put the comic down on the table and shut my eyes tight.

At that moment the door opened. From the sickening waft

of aftershave, I knew straight away that it was Ste. I opened one eye, being careful not to look at Mum or Dad.

"Hey hey hey. Mum, Dad, Freak. Just heading out for the morning," he said, smiling as though nothing was wrong.

He did not even bat an eyelid.

Our mum and dad were eating breakfast. In the nude. With no clothes on. And he did not even care. This was unbelievable. What was the world coming to?

"Oh, Steven, sit down and have some breakfast with us," said Mum, taking a bowl and a spoon from the piles in the middle of the table like it was the most normal thing in the world. "We haven't seen you all week."

Did I mention that everyone, including my mum and dad, thinks Ste is brilliant?

Ste shrugged. "What can I say? The Stevenator has been getting busy with a lucky young lady called Lucy King."

Mum tittered as she poured cornflakes into her bowl. "Oh, Steven. It's not Lucy King from the swimming club, is it? Dave King's daughter? He's a lovely man."

Mum has always had a soft spot for Dave King. She always chats to him after I have finished training. I do not understand why, though. In my opinion he is one of the most unpleasant people on Earth.

"Well," said Ste, "it's not *him* I'm interested in."

Mum giggled. "Well, Lucy *is* very pretty. Michael's got a picture of her on his wall, you know."

"I have not!" I snapped. "It is a newspaper cutting. I cut it out because the article mentions my name.[25] I just could not be bothered to remove the photo."

"Of Lucy King," said Mum.

Ste laughed at me. "Hey hey hey, is that right, bum fluff? I'll let her know she's got a fan. Or should I say a stalker. You know, Mum, Mike and Roly Poly Paul got kicked out of training yesterday for spying on her in her swimming cossie. Laters, everyone."

He winked at me as he walked out.

Mum clinked her spoon down in her bowl. "Is that right, Michael? Well, that says a lot, doesn't it, Roy?"

Dad grunted.

"I thought that you were embarrassed by the human form," she said, warming to the subject. "Turns out you're just a peeping Tom. Well, it seems to me that you need to accept the fact that people have bodies, Michael. We've all got them and it's nothing to be ashamed of or smutty about. Then you won't be so uptight all the time, shutting your eyes or spying on girls."

I opened my eyes in sheer frustration, staring hard at my half-finished cereal. "I was not spying on her. It was Paul."

---

25 Taken from the *Evening News* local sports section last June on the day after Lucy broke six club records in the Preston Piranhas Swimming Club championships. Before my race I slipped off the block and smacked my head on the poolside, delaying the races by half an hour. The headline reads: "King is the Queen as Court Jester Breaks his Crown".

Mum tutted. "Why would Ste say it, then? I wish you were more laid-back like him. Notice how he didn't make a fuss when he saw us. Now can I have the milk?"

I sat there seething.

"Fine," she said, "I'll get it myself."

What Happened Next, AKA The Absolute Worst Moment of My Entire Life Part III

1. She stood up slightly.
2. She leaned over the table, right in front of me.
3. She reached out for the milk.
4. This horrifying chain of events caused her *boob* to dangle into my Coco Pops.

Her boob.

In my *Coco Pops*, for heaven's sake.

I could not believe it. It just hung there in my breakfast like some kind of hungry sea cow. I could not speak. I could not even move.

She sat back down and poured the milk into her bowl like nothing had happened. She had not even noticed. There was a dripping sound as the milk made a puddle on the table.

I pushed my bowl away, a cold sweat beading on my forehead.

"Not hungry, Michael?"

"No. I will get something later."

I stood up and left the room.

Chatting With Chas

Session 2 Transcript

People present and location as Session 1[26]

Chas: Yo, Mikey.

MS: Do I have to be here?

Chas: No, man. No way. You can go any time you want.

MS: Oh, good. Thank you.

[MS stands up, removes microphone and exits room.]

[End of transcript]

26 Chas was wearing rose-tinted circular sunglasses and a loud T-shirt with a slogan that read: "Chillax to the Max".

Dealing With Feelings Session 7

When I arrived today, there was no glass of squash, no biscuit and no smile. The laptop was out on the table and Miss O'Malley did not even look at me when I came in.

"So, I heard what happened yesterday at the university," she said, still not looking at me, as I sat down. "Chas was very upset."

I paused. "He told me I could leave."

Miss O'Malley harrumphed and slammed her massive fist down on her desk. "Do you know, young man," she said, composing herself, "you're not the only person in the world to have problems?"

"My parents are NUDISTS," I said angrily. "They shamed me in front of the whole town. My brother stole and ruined the most impressive athlete in the entire county. I have got flipping issues coming out of my flipping ears. What on Earth could honestly be worse than that?"

Miss O'Malley pursed her lips. "It's not a competition, Michael, but other people have difficulties too. Growing up is hard."

"You sound like that book, *My Body is Changing.*"

"And a fine book it is too."

I rolled my eyes at this. It is in fact the worst book of all time.

There was a long pause before Miss O'Malley gave a big sigh. "Look, Michael, I'm sorry I snapped at you. And I suppose I should be glad you're speaking to me at all."

I shrugged.

Miss O'Malley took a deep breath. "Ah, Michael. When I was your age, people used to tease me, you know. Because of these."

She held up her gigantic paws. I swear the room got darker, like during a solar eclipse. I gulped.

"I blame my daddy, Michael. He kept horses, you see."

I instantly recoiled. "Horses. Yuck."

"Well, what's wrong with horses, Michael?"

I felt my face getting red. "It is not just horses. It is more donkeys, actually. I do not trust anything with hooves, though. My brother did something once when I was having a donkey ride. That is all."

"Oh yes. I think you might have mentioned it in your writing. Something you want to talk about now?" she said, raising her eyebrows.

When I shook my head, she paused for a moment before she carried on talking. "You should talk more. You're getting better, but you need to open up. Now, where was I? Oh yes. My hands. Now you may have noticed they're a little, well, large."

"No. I have not noticed that," I lied.

Miss O'Malley tutted and wagged one of her salami fingers at me. "Oh now, Michael, pull the other one. It's got bells on it. I *have* read the things you've been typing on the laptop, you know."

I looked at the floor. I did not wish to make her feel bad about herself.

"Ah well," she continued, "everyone in my family has big hands. My daddy had big hands, my mammy had big hands. Oh God, even my granny had hands like dustbin lids, you know. So it was no surprise when I came into the world with big hands too."

I shrugged again.

"But that was not the problem, you see. I mean, people might not skit you for hands that are just *big*. I don't think people really notice hands like they notice faces. The problem with hands comes when they draw attention to themselves.

"You see, I used to *love* helping my daddy with the horses. Mucking out the stables, tacking, grooming, I did *everything*. I was down there in all weather, working till my back ached and my fingers were red raw. Now, the problem is, if you work like that all the time, your hands are going to get strong and rough, like a workman.

"Like I say, I had big old hams anyway but, cos I worked with the horses all the time, my skin was always rough, my nails were cracked and split, my knuckles were gnarled. I had calluses on top of calluses and my fingers were *muscular*. I bet you didn't know you could get muscular fingers, but there you go. Back then I was a wee slip of a girl as well, so it was even worse. I might as well have worn a sign round my neck saying 'Come and look at the humongous hands'.

"Now, even though my hands were, well, *unusual*, I didn't really pay any attention to them until one day." She took a deep breath and whistled hard. "A boy at school asked me to go to the pictures with him. Now I was excited. No boys ever took notice of me, you know. And this wasn't any boy, this was Callum McCormack, only the most popular boy in the whole year."

A nasty, sicky, sinking feeling built up in my stomach. I did not think that this story would have a happy ending.

Miss O'Malley took a deep, sad breath. "So, anyway, I had never made myself up before, you know, so I got my mammy to help me. She was clucking and laughing and saying I looked like a princess and my daddy dropped me off round the corner from the cinema and said that wasn't I the prettiest girl in all of Ireland. Anyway, so there I was in this gorgeous dress and I walked up to the front door and Callum was there, looking all cool with his hands behind his back. And my heart skipped a beat. I thought he must be hiding some flowers for me, you know, like those romantic men in the films." A faint smile played on her lips. It soon disappeared. "Then I walked right up to him and said hello and then before I knew it, all of his friends were standing around me with big grins on their faces and all of them had *their* hands behind *their* backs too. And I said, 'What's going on?' because wasn't that a funny thing. Then Callum and the others suddenly pulled their hands out from behind their backs and. . ."

"What happened?" I said, a lump in my throat.

"Well. They all had on these big rubber gloves, you know, for washing up, but they'd stuffed them full of newspaper or something so they were bulging out and massive. And they started laughing at me and slapping me on the head and face with the horrible rubbery fingers and neighing like horses and calling me manky hands and sausage fingers and asking if I scooped up the manure with a shovel or just used my hands and all that rubbish and I didn't know what I'd done or nothing but I couldn't get out because they were all around me."

She swept something out of her eye.

"What did you do?" I said.

She composed herself for a second. "I took one look at that Callum, laughing his stupid head off at me stood there like an idiot in my best dress, and I cried and cried and ran home and couldn't tell me mammy or daddy what had happened or anything. All I knew was I had to do something.

"So the next Monday at school, I saw Callum and his friends laughing and waving their hands about, reliving the big joke to everyone in my class, but they hadn't seen me, right, so I walked over. . ."

"And?"

Her face stiffened. "I punched the little gobshite right in the mouth and smashed his bleedin' teeth out."

I almost fell off my chair with the ferocity of it all. She had completely transformed. Her eyes were burning hot and her teeth were bared like a rabid wolf.

"Then I cracked a couple of the others round the chops before they all ran off." She took a deep breath to compose herself and returned almost instantly to the soft, quiet person I knew. "Now that day I decided two things:

1. No more boys for me.
2. No more taking rubbish off anyone.[27]

"And that, young Michael, is that. Now, you need to understand something here. I had a tough time. A horrible time. But I faced up to it. I said these weren't lessons but I'm trying to teach you something now. You *need* to face up to this. I think there are reasons why you got so . . . you know . . . worked up about everything that happened. I can only do so much for you. You need a real expert to help you get down to the nitty-gritty. I think Chas can do that. He knows more about this stuff than me."

"He wears stupid clothes, though."

Miss O'Malley sighed. "I know he does, but he's *brilliant*, Michael, and he'll help you. The thing is, though, that the only way you can sort this all out is if *you* can help *yourself*. Do you understand? I can't do anything more for you on my own. I got you talking, I suppose, and writing things down, but this is going to be the last Dealing With Feelings session we're going to have."

---

27 I had to admire her use of a list here.

"What?"

"Yes, I've spoken to the school and your mum. They're happy about it. From tomorrow you're going to meet with Chas here instead. He says he's dead keen to come to the school because he thinks you're very special. Hopefully he can thaw out your brain freeze and get you to find a bit of peace. Keep the laptop. Keep writing things down. I think it's helping you a lot."

I felt my face crinkling up into a frown.

"Now don't look like that. I'll be here with you every day when he comes in. And you can come and see me whenever you need a quiet place or someone to talk to. But, from now on, it's Chas who'll be helping you most. Not me."

"Good grief," I said.

This was not good.

I do not feel like writing anything else today.

Chatting With Chas

Session 3 Transcript

People present at Session 1, plus Miss Patricia O'Malley (hereafter POM)

Location

Woodplumpton Village College, Preston

Chas: Yo. Mikey. The Mike-ster. Mikerooni cheese.

MS: Michael.

[Forty-five-second pause.]

POM: Michael prefers to be called Michael.

Chas: Oh. A-*hem*. Sorry, Michael. What's in a name, huh?

MS: [*Shrugs shoulders.*]

Chas: Oh. Well. Let's get straight down to it. This whole thing is about your parents, right?

MS: Correct. Mainly my mother.

Chas: So what's the beef? Did you ever feel let down by her? Y'know. Dare I say it, unloved?

[Three-minute pause.]

MS: She did not seem to notice my feelings, that is all.

Chas: Bingo, baby. We've locked down the mother load.

MS: What?

POM: [*Whispering to Chas behind her hand.*] Is it appropriate to speak like that in front of him, Chas? You know, he is a very delicate boy.

Chas: [*Whispering to POM behind his hand.*]

Chill, Miss O'Malley. Michael doesn't mind.

MS: I do mind.[28]

[Thirty-second pause.]

Chas: Oh. Still. That's great stuff, big man. All great stuff. Feel like we're getting under your skin. Let's cool it for now, though. We can take this puppy up to Mach 3 next time.

MS: What *are* you talking about?

Chas: [*Sound of fingers clicking.*] That's a wrap, peeps.

MS: What? Already?

Chas: Gotta split. Laters.[29]

[End of transcript]

After Chatting With Chas

Chas has gone. I am glad. I cannot believe they let him into the school. He is an idiot. Here are some things that irritated me today:

---

28 I have no idea why they bothered to whisper to each other. I was sitting two feet away, for heaven's sake.

29 At this point, he swept up his digital sound recorder, kissed Miss O'Malley on the hand and skateboarded out of the room. Yes, he had a skateboard with him.

1. His clothes (again). At this session, he was wearing a hooded top which had the words "Urban Gorilla" on it, along with a picture of a gorilla spraying graffiti on a wall. This was just about his stupidest item of clothing yet. A) Gorillas cannot use spray cans and B) even if they could I am certain that they would not turn into vandals.
2. His beard. It used to be bad enough but today he had shaved lightning bolts into each side of it.
3. His smell. Now that he has left, the room smells of beans. I had not noticed it before today but now I realize that he *stinks* of baked beans. It is the strangest personal odour I have ever noticed.
4. He keeps leering at Miss O'Malley. Today he even brought her a bunch of flowers. *Flowers*. He gives me the creeps.

Since he left, Miss O'Malley has been fussing around her flowers and whistling like a toothless sailor. I do not like this one bit.

What Happened After the Coco Pops Incident

After Mum had ruined my breakfast by invading my cereal bowl, the rest of that day went pretty badly. Mum and Dad spent most of the morning out in the garden, totally nude. I swear that Paul

Beary called round fourteen times before midday. Each time, he would stand at the front door trying to look over my shoulder into the back garden whilst I told him that, no, he could not come in and see my mum. In the middle of the afternoon, I decided to get out and go for a bike ride. As I pushed my bike along the path behind our house, I found Paul trying to climb our back fence, his mobile phone clenched between his teeth.

Luckily, Mum and Dad had already gone inside by this time, after Dad got stung by a bee in a very sensitive place.

This was not the point, though.

"What are you doing?" I yelled.

Paul slipped, landing in a heap on the ground and dropping his phone. He got up and dusted himself off. "Yeah. I was . . . er . . . just calling for you."

Paul is a terrible liar. Apart from the gems I mentioned earlier, in the ten years I have known him, he has also told me the following things:

1. He was once shot in the head with an air rifle. Although he was unhurt, the pellet (which miraculously left no mark on entry) remains lodged in his brain and allows him to pick up Radio 1 inside his skull.
2. Last year he saw two ninjas fighting in Moor Park (no mention of *why* the ninjas were there) on a Sunday afternoon. Apparently, one of them died when the

other frisbee'd a bin lid straight through his heart.

3. One day he was eating a sausage roll (nothing strange about the story so far) when he discovered a human finger inside it (knowing the food in the school canteen, there is still nothing strange about the story so far). Just as he was about to scream, however, the finger started beckoning to him. He dropped the sausage roll in horror and the finger slithered away.[30]

Anyway, I told Paul that this was a load of rubbish. "You were obviously trying to take pictures of my mum. Admit it."

"No," he said, his eyes looking like they were about to pop out.

At that moment, his phone beeped. It was lying by my foot so I picked it up. There was a text message from someone called "Turdo".

I read it out to him. "'Yo Beary. When U sendin dem nudey pics? U got 10 mins or I want my money back.'

"*Which* pictures exactly, Paul?" I said, shoving the phone into his chest.

Paul took the phone in his chubby hand and began examining it sheepishly. "Yeah. They're some other pictures. He wanted pictures of, erm. . ."

My blood was pumping so hard it felt like my eyeballs were

---

30 I do not know what is more unbelievable – finding a severed finger with a mind of its own inside a sausage roll or Paul throwing food away.

going to explode. "Pictures of what, Paul? Fighting ninjas? Your French girlfriend? Your auntie's caravan?"

"Uncle's," he said, looking hurt.

"Whatever. I know what you were doing, and do you know what? You have gone too far. It is bad enough *you* trying to cop an eyeful of my mum in the nude, let alone having you sell the pictures to someone called *Turdo*. Just stay away from us, you reprobate."

I cycled off as fast as I could.

"She wouldn't do it if she didn't want people to see her," he called behind me as I disappeared round the corner.

I tried not to believe him.

An Unexpected Guest

I rode for about two hours out into the countryside. I like cycling. It gets me away from other people. Your feet just go round and round so there are no surprises. On the way back I bought some custard creams to cheer myself up.

When I got home, tired and a little sweaty, I cautiously opened the lounge door. Luckily, Mum and Dad were not there.

Ste was sitting in the armchair, feet up on the coffee table. This was almost as bad as seeing Mum or Dad at the moment.

Then I saw who else was sitting on the sofa.

"Great Scott," I said. "Lucy."

Lucy smiled sweetly. I guess that she was not still mad about me and Paul spying on her. Not that *I* had been spying on her, of course.

Ste clicked his fingers and pointed at me. "Take a seat, lil' bro."

There was only one space left. Next to Lucy. I gulped.

"C'mon, Mikester. She won't bite. Unless she likes you."

Lucy pretended to be shocked and reached forward to slap Ste on the leg. My face burned. How dare he say that to her? A top athlete like her deserves some respect. I felt the custard creams getting warm in my hands.

Nervously, I sat down next to Lucy on the sofa. It is only a two-seater so I was crushed up so close to her that our bare legs were touching. I could feel my skin start to prickle. A warm sweat was sticking my T-shirt to my back.

"Sorry about yesterday," I squeaked.

"Don't worry about it. I know it wasn't you who was spying on me," Lucy said, brushing an imaginary piece of dust off her leg. Her fingernails *almost* touched my knee. "It was that other one. You know, the *large* boy who's always lurking around outside the girls' toilets at school."

I nodded. This was a very accurate and concise description of Paul Beary.

"Mikey's a big fan of yours, Luce," Ste said.

"Aww," Lucy said.

"What?" I said.

Ste reached over her to ruffle my hair. "Yeah. He's always talking about what a great swimmer you are."

"Thanks, Mike," Lucy said.

"Yeah, but. . ." I said.

Ste gave one of his nasty smiles. "He's even got a picture of you in your costume on his wall."

"Oh," Lucy said. "Bit strange."

"I can explain. It is a newspaper article. I am mentioned in it," I said, beginning to wheeze a little.

"Well, yeah, Mike," said Ste, "it mentions you as, and I quote, 'a clumsy clown who toppled off his diving block, much to the amusement of the astonished spectators'."

Lucy sniggered. "Hang on. That was at the club championships, wasn't it. Oh my God. Was that *you*?"

"Yes," I said, my skin smouldering and my breathing becoming more rapid. "A) I was nervous, B) I had not eaten, C) there were a lot of people there staring at me and D) someone must have put grease on my block to make it slippery."

"Aw," said Lucy, as though I was some kind of penguin that needed to be put down.

Apart from my heavy asthma breathing, silence descended on the room. I took a puff on my inhaler.

After a while, Ste coughed and picked up a saucer from the table. There were biscuits on it. "Bourbon cream, Michael? I see that you've brought the cheapskate version. Fancy something with a bit more class?"

Bourbon creams! The cheek of it!

Lucy smiled and gripped his hand. "Kind to his little brother as well. What more could a girl ask for?"

My hands were so hot, it felt like my custard creams were about to go up in flames. I was starting to wheeze hard. Trust Ste to try to outdo me with a jazzier biscuit. Everyone knows that custard creams are in fact better, though. Such a *Ste* thing to do: try to impress everyone with the obvious choice. Classy people always prefer custard creams. Idiots like Ste are the only people who prefer Bourbons.

Now was my chance.

I took a shallow, tickly breath and smiled at Lucy. "Well, I happen to have these here, if anyone would like a choice."

Welcome to my world, Ste.

I thrust the packet of custard creams towards Lucy like a fencing sword and gave Ste a little knowing grin. Did I detect him looking a little worried? Ha! He knew when he was beaten.

"No, thank you, Mike," Lucy smiled, sweetly. "Actually, I'm only allowed one biscuit a week and I've already eaten a Bourbon cream. They're my favourites."

Damn.

"Oh, one will not hurt," I said, hopefully.

"That's not what my dad says," said Lucy.

Ste tutted. "As if he'll ever know."

"You don't know him. He weighs me every Monday and gives me a monthly body fat test. He says, what with the Guild gala and the Nationals coming up, I can't afford to slack off for a minute."

"Sounds like a right Hitler," groaned Ste.

"You cannot say that," I snapped, even though I knew he was right. Lucy was wincing.

"Well, he does," Ste said, waving his hand at me dismissively. "Bossing you around like that. Enjoy yourself, Lucy. You're with the Stevenator. Have a biscuit."

"I don't know about that," she said.

"Custard creams have fewer calories," I offered.

Ste scoffed. "Don't have a custard cream, babe; they're for old people and tramps. Have a Bourbon."

I glared at him but he had pulled his phone out to check a text. He smiled to himself before shoving it back into his pocket.[31]

Lucy pursed her lips. Slowly, she began to smile. "Oh, OK. What he can't see won't hurt him."

She scoffed the Bourbon quickly, her eyes flicking nervously from side to side as though her dad were watching her. "Now I've really got to get out of here. I've got two hours in the gym before training tonight. Will you be there, Mike?"

I nodded as hard as I could. "Yes, I think I will. Number one, I've got the Guild gala, and number two, I want to get in shape

---

31 Is there any point in mentioning that of course Ste has the best phone you can buy? He won it in a raffle at school the other month because it was being drawn by a girl on the student council who fancies him. My phone, however, is one of Mum's old ones. It has a cracked screen and is about the size of a man's shoe.

so I will look my best on the float at the torchlit procession."

Lucy raised her eyebrows. "You're going to be on the float? Me too."

"Yes. Your dad invited me. I will be a sea slug," I said, proudly. "I will be protecting you as the queen of the ocean." I gave Ste a sly smile at this point.

Ste rolled his eyes in response. "Come on, babe. We've got to get off. I'm playing football with the lads."

"But you have not played football since you broke your leg," I said.

Ste glared at me. "Yes. Well, now I'm playing again."

He basically yanked her out of the door as she tried to say goodbye to me. Typical Ste.

The Best Training Session Ever

Later on, I went to the pool for the Sunday night training session. It is never as good as Saturday because the swimming club has the whole pool booked and my lane is right over the far side from Lucy's.

Before the session, I walked along the poolside, trying to avoid my mum's eyes from up on the balcony. Lucy said hello to me and shared a joke about goggle marks that made me laugh a little bit too much.

Then Dave King came along and told me I sounded like a

mental patient and that I should shut up and stop distracting the elite swimmers when they had a big gala to prepare for. At this point, Lucy winked at me. Yes, you read that correctly, she winked at me.

Things that a wink can mean:

1. Something that baddies in films do to show they are about carry out a sinister act against the person they are winking at without telling them what it is.
2. A shared joke that nobody else is supposed to know about.
3. A cheeky gesture to show you like someone.
4. A twitch.

I was pretty certain that Lucy's wink was either 2 or 3 and definitely not 1 or 4. If it was number 3 then that was quite simply brilliant. If it was number 2 then that could mean that it was also number 3 anyway. I mean, who would share a joke with someone they did not like.[32]

After Lucy dived in Dave asked me if the little weasel sniffing round Lucy was my brother. I said yes and he said well wasn't that a surprise and maybe my whole family was

---

32 By "like", I definitely do not mean "fancy". I would not have wanted Lucy to spoil our friendship by fancying me. We were now officially friends, after all. I mean, we *had* just had a conversation.

genetically programmed to destroy his and Lucy's chance of glory. I laughed weakly and he told me that it wasn't a joke and I should get in the water otherwise he'd kick me so hard up the arse I'd be flushing toenails down the toilet for the rest of my life. I did not care, though. Throughout the whole session I whizzed through the water knowing that Lucy King, elite athlete and all-round brilliant person, had winked at me.

Chatting With Chas

Session 4 Transcript

People present and location as Session 3

Chas: Yo, Mikey. Great to see you.

MS: Oh.

Chas: OK, babe. Let's get started. You know, I got something that's been busting my chops, you dig?

MS: No.

Chas: It's like this, dude. I read your stuff, you know, off the laptop.

MS: Yes, I know.

Chas: All the time, you notice tiny details about everyone. Except for your parents.

MS: So.

Chas: So these are like the worst things you've ever seen and you can't describe 'em. You know how many verrucas there are on your friend Paul's foot.

MS: Nineteen.

POM: He's right. I've treated him. His big toe looks like a cauliflower.

Chas: Nice. But the thing is, nowhere in your writing does it say anything about what your parents look like.

[Five-second pause.]

MS: Both early forties. Mum blonde. Dad balding. Both hideous when nude.

Chas: Cool. But you know what I think? That shows me you're afraid. Shows me we gotta get to the bottom of what's going on in your skull, you get me? I'm gonna show you some pics. You tell me what they make you think of.

MS: Hmm. What are they pictures of?

Chas: Nothing, bud. Nothing at all. They're abstract. You just tell me what you see. You dig?

[Shows first picture.]

MS: Donkey.

Chas: Hmmm.

[Shows second picture. Two-minute pause.]

MS: Do I have to do this?

Chas: Why do you ask that? What's the beef?

MS: Just because.

Chas: Something freaking you out about the picture, big dude?

[Thirty-second pause.]

MS: No.

Chas: Sure?

[One-minute pause.]

MS: I need the toilet.

Chas: Sure, babe. A man's gotta do what a man's gotta do.

[MS exits.]

Chas: [*To POM.*]

OK. I'll bet my DJ decks[33] that this little piggy's going to market.

POM: I'm awfully sorry. I don't quite understand.

Chas: He's getting out quick. He's making an escape. He ain't coming back, baby.[34]

POM: Oh really?

Chas: Dur. Yeah. And do you wanna know why? Something about that picture. It reminded him of something.

---

33 Yes. You read this correctly. DJ decks.

34 Although it pains me to say it, he was right about this. I actually went and hid in the toilets for the rest of the hour.

POM: What like?

Chas: Dunno. Probably something about his parents in the nude.[35] I told you, this is one messed up kid. What's all this crazy talk about a donkey, anyway?

POM: Oh. I don't know.

[Five-second pause.]

Actually, he mentioned something before. He doesn't like them. He doesn't trust anything with hooves. Oh yes. Something his brother did.

Chas: Yoink. We'll lay down *that* groove tomorrow.

POM: What?

Chas: Forget it, sweet thing. Let's call it a wrap.

POM: [*Laughs.*]

Sweet thing. You *are* awful!

[End of transcript]

The Picture

I had to get out of that place. The pictures were just black splodges on a white background but I did not like them. The first one looked like an angry donkey. And the second? Well, I do

35 Unfortunately, he was right about this as well.

not like to mention what it looked like,but let's just say it reminded me of Coco Pops. And not in a good way. I have brought the laptop to the school library. Nobody will disturb me here.

Paul's Olive Branch

On the Monday after the Best Swimming Session of My Life, I was sitting at the back of Miss Skinner's art lesson, trying to draw some flowers. They looked more like sausages.

"Oh yes, Michael," Miss Skinner said, as she floated past me. I mentioned her earlier. She is the art teacher with the goss eyes and the moustache. Unfortunately, she plays a large role in this story. "Perfect. Don't just draw what you see. Draw the *essence* of the flower. Draw what you imagine the flower is trying to say to you."

I had no idea what she was on about, unless the flower was trying to say "I belong on a plate with some mashed potato."

"Er. Thanks."

"Oh yes," she said, "and tell your mother she's *very* welcome at my adult art class tomorrow after school. So good to have parents who wish to get involved."

"OK," I said, confused. *Adult art class?* Since when had my mum been interested in art? I hardly felt like I knew her any more. Still, as long as it stopped her from doing her other hobbies. . .

"Pssst!" came a voice from the next table. I looked up. Paul Beary was trying to get my attention, crisp crumbs spraying out of his mouth like sparks out of a cheap firework.

"What do you want?" I muttered back to him.

"Aw, come on, Mike," he whispered. "Look. I'm sorry. I'll make it up to you after this lesson, I promise."

"Quiet, back there," said Miss Skinner, her eyes looking in two completely different directions. "Do not try to interrupt the mystical flow of artistic endeavour, Mr Beary."

"Sorry, miss," said Paul.

"And by the way, Mr Beary, your flowers look more like sausages."

I was not sure if she was looking at Paul's picture or mine. It must be very confusing when you are always looking in two different directions.

Operation Birdseye

After art, Paul led me down the stairs and over the playground to the far side of the gymnasium, right on the edge of the school grounds. It is a place where not many people go unless they are up to something they should not be doing.

"Where are we going?" I said. "We are meant to be in RE in two minutes."

"Huh," said Paul, checking the coast was clear before dragging me down the little gap between the breeze-block wall of the gym and the boundary fence of the school. "Careful of the nettles down here. They're a pain but they keep other people out."

In the distance I could hear high-pitched laughter.

"What do you mean, keep other people out?" I said nervously, as I inched my way past a razor-sharp bramble. The pathway is so overgrown that not even the tough kids come down here when they want to smoke.

Paul came to a sudden stop and pointed to a small open window above him. I realized that this was where the laughter was coming from, carried on clouds of steam.

"The girls' changing rooms?" I said. I did not like the sound of this one bit.

Paul put his hand on my shoulder. His face was intensely serious. "This is to say sorry. I've never shown this to anyone before. Welcome to Operation Birdseye."

"Operation Birdseye? What are you going to do? Cook fish fingers?"

Paul shook his head. "Don't be thick. I checked the timetable. Year 11 PE has just finished and you know what that means. . ."

"No."

Paul slapped me on the back of the head. "Lucy King. She'll be in there getting dressed right now."

"And. . ."

Paul pulled a fruit pastille from his pocket and shoved it into his mouth. "Have a look at this."

He reached behind him and pulled a ladder out from amongst the nettles.

"Where on Earth did you get that?" I said.

"Library," he winked. "I nicked it last year."

"Last year? How often do you come down here?"

Paul sniffed. "Oh, not too often. Couple of times a day. I've been cutting down recently."

"Cutting down? How often did you used to come here?"

Paul bit his lip. "Remember last year when I was off school ill for three days?"

I nodded. "You told me you had the Black Death."

"Yeah," said Paul, nudging some pebbles round on the floor with his foot. "Well, let's just say I wasn't ill."

"What? You were here for three days solid? How come you never told me?"[36]

"Top secret," he said tapping his nose. "You're only here now cos I want to say sorry. Now up you go."

"What do you mean?"

Paul rolled his eyes. "Mike. The girl you fancy is on the other side of that window soaping herself up as we speak. You've got to get up there. Millions of people would kill to be in on Operation Birdseye."

---

36 I felt strangely left out, even though I did not really want to be there.

"Well I am not one of them. This is disgusting. All those naked bodies. And I do not *fancy* her," I hissed, "I *admire* her and *respect* her. In any case, Miss Skinner's window overlooks this place. We could get caught."

"Oh, come on. Old cross-eyed Skinner couldn't see us if she was stood right here. Now if you're not going up there to *admire* and *respect* her, I am."

With that, he shoved the ladder up against the wall and started climbing it. I looked on in horror as he reached the top and poked his head through the little window. "Perfect timing," he whispered.

There was a shriek from inside the changing rooms. Suddenly a face emerged through the steam at the window. It was Brutus the Beefcake – the huge girl from the swimming club.

"Oh no," said Paul. "Gorilla in the mist."

"You again," growled Brutus.

Paul Gets His Comeuppance and, As Usual, I Come Off Badly Too

Now the thing about a headbutt is that it all happens so quickly. So quickly, in fact, that Paul did not have time to duck. Before either of us knew what was happening, he was lying on top of me on the ground, clutching his bleeding nose. Above us, the window slammed shut.

"Michael Swarbrick. Paul Beary," came a cry from towards the main school building. We slowly stood up. Miss Skinner was leaning out of her window on the first floor. "Disgusting. Detention. After school tomorrow. Parents will be informed."

Great.

I guess her eyes were not that bad after all.

Mum Finds Out

That evening, Mum opened the letter and theatrically cleared her throat. "So what have we here? Ooh, it's from Miss Skinner. 'Michael was caught spying today on the Year 11 girls getting changed and will tomorrow be kept in an after-school detention.' Spying? There's a surprise. Lucy King, by any chance? It's a wonder her father isn't after you."

Ste shook his head. "I told you, Mum. He's a sick individual and he must be stopped."

"Anything you want to say, Roy?" Mum said to Dad.

Dad grunted and tucked into his shepherd's pie.

"Thanks for that," she said, sarcastically. "Now don't tell me, Michael, it was Paul Beary again, wasn't it."

"Yes!" I said.

Mum rolled her eyes. "You can't keep blaming him for everything."

"Yeah," said Ste, chipping in unnecessarily, "as if Elephant Boy could get up a ladder like that."

At that point Ste's phone rang.

"Yo yo yo, Lovely Lucy. How's it going, babe? Tomorrow? No can do, I'm afraid. Plans. The guys. Poker. Boy stuff. What's wrong with tonight? Forget about training. You go every day. One session ain't gonna hurt. Forget your dad. Tell him you're sick and Doctor Stevenator has got some sweet medicine for you. OK. OK. OK. Sorry, babe. Yeah, I understand. Well, let's hang out for a few hours before you go. Call me. Mwah."

"You do not play poker," I said, after he had hung up. "And anyway, she has got the Guild gala and the Nationals coming up. You should not be trying to get her to miss training."

"Oh go spy on someone, Lames Bond."

The door slammed behind him.

"Now see what you've done," said Mum, slamming down her knife and fork. "You fear the human body, you fear nudity, yet you spy on girls getting changed for cheap thrills and offend people who are having a normal teenage relationship. How did you turn out like this?"

I put my elbows on the table and rested my head in my hands. This was too much to handle.

Detention

Detention the next day was not too bad. This is because:

1. We just had to sharpen colouring pencils in Miss Skinner's room. I like doing this as I prefer it when all of the pencils are the same sharpness.
2. Paul brought a packet of Rolos with him. They were soft and warm because he had kept them in his pocket all day. Still, they were better than nothing. He must have felt bad about me being in detention because he even let me have two.[37]
3. Miss Skinner barely looked at us once so we were able to chat the whole time. She spent the entire hour rearranging a bed sheet on a table in the middle of the room, staring at it with her wonky eyes, then tutting and rearranging it again.

At the end of the hour, Paul asked if we could leave. Miss Skinner was swinging the bed sheet around her head like a hammer thrower. She let go, flinging it through the air so that it billowed down over the table. She clapped her hands

37 These lasted me the whole hour because I know how to pace myself. Paul scoffed the rest three at a time and the packet was finished within about a minute.

together and giggled. "Perfect," she twittered, even though A) it looked exactly the same as it did before and B) she actually appeared to be looking at a painting of a woman with an absurdly long neck on the far wall.

She gave us a dismissive wave. "Begone, vile cretins. The adult art class is about to commence."

Adult art class? Why did that ring a bell?

The Terrible Reason Why the Adult Art Class Rang a Bell

I walked out of the room and stopped dead in my tracks. My mum and dad were standing in the middle of the corridor. They were wearing dressing gowns.

"Oh, hello, Michael," Mum smiled. "Hello, Paul."

"Hi, Mrs Swarbrick. What a lovely surprise," said Paul. "Is that a silk robe you're wearing?"

I elbowed him in the stomach. It was like sinking my arm into a giant marshmallow. I almost had to use my other hand to help remove it.

"What are you doing here?" I asked, pulling Mum to one side. "And why are you both dressed like . . . that?"

"Art class," sighed Mum. "Remember? You failed to pass on the message from Miss Skinner yesterday, as you were too busy spying on girls. Luckily she included it as a 'PS' in the letter she sent me about your little indiscretion."

At this moment, Miss Skinner wafted over to the doorway. "Oh welcome, welcome. How wonderful you could make it," she gushed, waving dramatically at the table with a sheet on it. "Your plinth awaits."

"Plinth? What is a plinth?" I said uneasily.

"A plinth," said Miss Skinner, speaking to me but looking at Paul, "is a raised object on which models prostrate themselves so that others might form an artistic likeness using whatever medium they so desire. Your parents have kindly agreed to be those models."

I looked from Miss Skinner to Mum, to Dad, and back to Miss Skinner again. "Models. What . . . *kind* of models?"

Dad stared at his feet. "Well, son, now that everything's in the open, your mother wanted us to come out and, well, go public. This wasn't my idea, you know."

"Oh be quiet, Roy," snapped Mum. "This is an art class. They advertised for models and we. . ."

"Well, it was more *you*," said Dad.

Mum shot him a dirty look, then faked a smile at a couple of people who were coming down the corridor holding pencil tins and easels. "Now if you'll excuse us, we must be getting ready. These dressing gowns won't take themselves off."

"Dressing gowns? Off?" I cried. "I hope you have got something else on underneath."

Mum raised an eyebrow. "Such as what, Michael? A fig leaf?"

I shuddered. "You are not going to. . . You do not mean. . . You could not. This has got to be against the law."

Mum took a step towards me. "They're our lives and our bodies and we'll do whatever we want."

"But this is my school," I whined. "People will see you."

"Only those people who are still here because they're in detention for spying on girls getting dressed."

With that she twirled around and flounced off into the room. Dad gave an apologetic shrug, then followed her inside, closing the door behind him.

"No, Paul," I said, "before you ask, we are *not* sticking around here for the next hour. And you can stop drooling as well."

Paul's shoulders dropped and he swore under his breath. When we walked round the corner, I had an even worse surprise waiting for me.

What Could Possibly Be Worse?

Walking towards me were Dave King and a woman who I guessed was Mrs King. Lucy's mum. As soon as he saw them, Paul dodged into an empty classroom. I guess he was still petrified after the incident at the swimming pool.

"Hello," I said nervously.

"Marvin," grunted Dave King.

"Is this one of the boys from the swimming club?" said Mrs King. She looked a bit like Lucy but much older. And her skin was bright orange. I guessed it was fake tan but it could easily be that stuff Dad uses to paint the garden fence. "Are you going to be doing the torchlit parade?"

"Yes. I am a sea slug. I will be protecting Lucy," I smiled.

"Wrong," growled Dave, "I'll be protecting Lucy. From that bloody brother of yours. Tell him from me that I know who he is and if he thinks he can jeopardize her career. . ."

Mrs King rolled her eyes. "Take no notice, Marvin. I'm sure your brother's a lovely boy and it's good for Lucy to have interests outside swimming."

Dave began counting to ten under his breath.

"Our Dave's a big pussycat really," smiled Mrs King. "We just need to calm him down a bit now and again. That's why we've taken up the art classes," she smiled, opening her handbag to show a set of pencils and a pad. "They fit in perfectly round Dave's coaching and get him nice and relaxed for the evening so he doesn't get too cross with the swimmers."[38]

Dave sniffed. "Got a problem with that?"

"No," I said, backing away a little. "It is just. You cannot go in there."

"I flaming well can," said Dave. "We're learning to draw people tonight."

---

38 This was definitely not working.

"Usually Dave just draws pictures of tanks and dismembered bodies," Mrs King said proudly.

"But the people," I said, putting my hand on Mrs King's arm and looking from side to side to make sure no one could hear me. "There is something you should know about them. They are . . . how can I say this? Naked."

Mrs King laughed. "Oh, don't be silly. We've seen plenty of naked people before. Dave, you didn't tell me there were such funny people at that swimming club of yours. Now it was very nice to meet you, Marvin. See you at the procession."

With that they walked straight past me.

They had seen plenty of naked people before?

What kind of oddballs have seen *plenty* of naked people before? How many is plenty, anyway? I had seen two in the last week and that was more than enough for me. Poor Lucy. I hoped that she had never had to look at naked people before as well.

Chatting With Chas

Session 5 Transcript

Location and people present as Session 3

Chas: Yo, Mikey. How's it hanging?

MS: How's what hanging?

Chas: Forget it, dude. Great to see you.

MS: They are making me come here.

Chas: Yeah. But I reckon you're starting to enjoy it.

[Twenty-second pause.]

Chas: So, yesterday, you did one. You legged it. You headed for the hills. What was with that?

[Forty-two-second pause.]

MS: I did not like the picture that you showed me.

Chas: I dig. I dig. Why not, man?

POM: Do we need to ask him this? He looks tired.

MS: I am. When you live in a tent it is hard to get a decent night's sleep.

[Ten-second pause.]

MS: I guess the picture reminded me of things that happened.

Chas: Miss O.M. tells me you hate donkeys.

MS: What has that got to do with anything?

Chas: You tell me.

MS: I was five. I went on the beach. I was riding a donkey. My brother scared it. It ran off with me on its back. I did not like it. I fell off. I hurt my chin. The end.

Chas: Are you sure?

MS: Course I am sure. Can I go? I need to put on some eczema cream. My hands are starting to flake.

Chas: Go for it, big chief. See you next time.

[Exit MS.]

Chas: Told you. There's something weird about that donkey thing. First thing he thinks about when he sees the pictures, but then he don't wanna talk about it. I'm gonna open his skull and see what's in his brains.

POM: Please don't.

Chas: Whoa, man. Figure of speech. Figure of speech. I ain't gonna do it for real, babe.

POM: Oh. Good.

Chas: Now how about we go get some lunch.

POM: Oh, thank you, but, erm, maybe not today. I, er, brought some sandwiches.

Chas: Right on, babe, right on. Next time.

[End of transcript]

On My Way Out of Chatting With Chas

I really did have to put cream on my hands, but I was glad of the excuse to get out of there. I did not want to talk about what happened with the donkey. I mean, that was nine years ago. What could it have to do with anything?

I was rushing away from the room when I suddenly ran

straight into Miss Skinner, almost knocking her over. She was really shocked to see me and kind of scuttled away like a frightened crab. She had only just managed to keep her job after everything that happened – probably only because the police did not press charges against her – and I guess she still blames me a bit.

I did not say sorry or even make sure she was all right. I just hurried into the toilets and hid for a while. Then, about two minutes ago, I crept back to Miss O'Malley's room. Before opening the door I pressed my ear against it to make sure that nobody was in the room. Luckily it was empty (I am guessing that Chas skated off straight after I left and that Miss O'Malley has been called away to deal with a nose bleed or something) so I slipped in and turned on the laptop.

Mum and Dad Return

At about 6:30 on that Tuesday, Mum and Dad came home from the art class. Mum was smiling broadly. Dad kind of shuffled in behind her.

"Oh, wasn't that just *liberating*," she announced. "All those years we've been building up to this day and finally we are out there in public. I feel like I've been released from prison."

"You should be put *in* prison," I mumbled. Dad and I shared a little smirk. He was definitely on my side. I was sure of it.

"What was that?" she snapped. She stared at me for a moment, then took a deep breath. A smile spread across her face. "You can't take the shine off this evening, Michael, so don't bother trying. I can't wait to do it again."

"Again?" said Dad and I at the same time. Dad looked even more horrified than I felt.

"Well, of course," said Mum, deadly serious. "This was a dry run. We've not been out into the fresh air yet. Except in the garden, of course, but that doesn't count. The more I think about it, the more I realize how stupid the world is."

"Stupid?" I said. This was a woman who had just spent two hours in the buff being drawn by Dave King.

"Yes," she said, "stupid. Why shouldn't I be nude where I want? Why have I had to lock myself up for nine years? I'll tell you why. Because *the law* says so. I've decided I am going to make a stand."

"But I thought that this would be it," said Dad. "We've tried it now. Surely we don't have to keep on doing it."

"We absolutely do," she said. "We've not even started. And I won't rest until we can proudly be ourselves without small-minded people thinking we're a pair of . . . of . . . of weirdos."[39]

"Please do not do this again. I beg you," I said.

"We'll do whatever we want," snorted Mum. "Anyway,

---

39 What kind of a weirdo would *not* think they were a pair of weirdos?

we'll talk about this later. I've got to say that Miss Skinner is a lovely lady. And the artists were so fantastic, especially Mr and Mrs King. Delightful couple. We had a great chat with them afterwards. Fabulous to see him away from the swimming pool. And so nice to finally meet his wife after all these years."

"I hope you put your dressing gowns on," I said.

Mum harrumphed. "No, Michael. They had been observing us in our natural states for an hour and a half. Obviously they are not prudish enough to be bothered about that sort of thing. They are *definitely* my kind of people. Anyway, get your swimming kit together. It's time for training."

Training

Training was awful that night. This is why:

1. Lucy was late, having been dropped off by my brother.
2. Because of 1, Dave was in a foul mood.[40] He made a big example of her in front of everyone, saying that the Guild gala was not going to be a walkover and she needed to knuckle down and work hard because French girls can swim like angry squids. Lucy just bowed her

40 Evidently the art class had not helped him with his anger management issues at all.

head and kept muttering "Yes, Dad" over and over again.

3. As a result of the bad temper mentioned in 2, Dave made us do thirty lengths of butterfly sprints. If you are not familiar with butterfly, it is an incredibly difficult and tiring swimming stroke invented in the Middle Ages as a means of torturing people. After about five minutes of this, I had to drag myself out on to the side and gulp down six puffs on my inhaler. Whilst I was lying there, breathless, on the cold hard tiles, Dave King "accidentally" trod on my fingers.
4. After training, I had to sit around for ages while Mum had a big long chat with Dave in the swimming pool foyer. I heard her make a really terrible joke which went something like, "Oooh, I bet you don't recognize me with my clothes on." This was the first time I had ever heard Dave laugh. She told him a load of rubbish about Ste being a nice boy and she would talk to him and make sure he didn't distract Lucy from her training any more and wouldn't it be lovely if they all met up sometime. Then the chat became noticeably more serious. They started muttering so quietly that I could not follow everything they were saying. Afterwards they exchanged mobile phone numbers. He said he would think about it (I did not quite catch what *it* was) and get back to her.

After all of this I was completely fed up. On the way home I asked her why she spent so much time talking to Dave King and why did she give him her phone number and why did she have to embarrass me all of the time by getting naked and fancying my swimming coach who is a maniac anyway.

She almost swerved the car off the road. "What did you say?"

I guess I had overstepped the mark.

Mum took a deep breath. "You have no idea, do you? If you must know, Mr King is a very nice man, not a maniac, and it is possible for two adults to be friends without 'fancying' each other. Your father and I found Dave and his wife to be very charming people and, despite his reservations about your brother, I am sure that our two families are going to be great friends."

"Why did you need to give him your mobile phone number, then, and what is Dad going to think about it?" I said.

Mum tutted and turned the radio on loudly.

Things Go From Really Bad to Even Worse

The following Friday after school, I was sitting in the front room, flicking through the channels on the TV. Mum was in the kitchen cooking tea. I was doing my best to avoid her because she was completely nude apart from an apron. That has got to be unhygienic. I had already decided that I was definitely not going to eat a single mouthful. Instead, I would polish off that packet of custard creams from the other day.

Since the art class a couple of days before, she had not worn clothes in the house once. All she went on about was how wonderful she felt and how liberating the whole thing was. In fact, on Wednesday she had wanted to wander down to the shops like that. *To the shops!* Dad had to beg her not to do it. He said it was illegal. She told him she would do what she liked and said that the law is an ass.

Ste said, "No, the law means you have to cover up your ass."[41]

The whole thing was getting out of hand. It was only a matter of time before she broke free.

Anyway, so there I was in the front room when the doorbell rang. Thinking that it was probably Paul Beary, who had been "just passing" about four times a day since he had seen Mum in the nude the week before, I hopped up and looked through the window.

It was Lucy King.

"Get that, please, Michael," called Mum from the kitchen.

This was a surprise. Ste had said he was going out to the

---

41 This is the second and last time that Ste ever made me laugh. The only reason I laughed this time was because it made Mum stop being silly and reluctantly put some clothes on. As it was Ste's joke, though, she even laughed herself. If I had said it, she would have probably grounded me.

cinema and I had guessed that he was going with Lucy.

Brilliant!

Maybe he had tried to squeeze her bottom in the darkness of the auditorium and she had dumped him and run back here to tell Mum what he was really like.

Disaster!

She could not see Mum like this.

I ran to the front door and opened it a tiny crack.

"Oh. Hi, Mike," said Lucy. She was carrying a large, flat parcel wrapped in brown paper under her arm. Her hair was wet from the pool and there were dark rings around her eyes.

"Hi, Lucy," I squeaked, poking my head through the gap in the door. "How are you?"

"Tired," she said, yawning. "Dad's still mad about me being late for training the other night. He's really making up for it now, though. The last few days have been murder. Extra sessions and everything. He's making me go to the gym tonight as well. Is Ste in?"

"Ste? Is he not with you?" I asked.

Lucy looked over her shoulders and pretended to look under the package, which was almost perfectly square. "Er. I don't think so."

I laughed a little bit too hard. "Ha ha! Obviously he is not. You are on your own."

I must have sounded demented.

Lucy took a step back. "Right. Do you know where he is? I

think his phone might be broken because I've not been able to get hold of him all day."

"Cinema," I said, "he is at the cinema. With friends." I have no idea why I added this bit. Ste had not mentioned anything about going out with his friends. It seemed a bit strange that Ste would be going to the cinema without Lucy, though, so I guess that I did not want her to ask too many questions.

"Oh, OK," she said. "Well, is your mum in?"

"No," I said, "she has gone."

"Gone?"

"Nu. . ." I almost said "nude" and had to quickly stop myself.

Lucy looked at me strangely. "New?"

"Yeah," I said. "New. New. New Zealand. That is it. She has gone to New Zealand."

"Really? Oh. That's nice. Well, my dad asked me to drop this off for her. He said it had something to do with his art class."

"Oh," I said. I looked at the parcel and realized at that moment what it was. "Oh no."

Lucy held it up. "You know, he's never let me look at any of his artwork before. He must be proud of this one, though, if he's put it in a frame. How come he's giving it to your mum?"

"You do not want to know," I said.

A little cheeky look crept on to Lucy's face. "Oh, Mike. I'm dying to have a look. You don't mind if I come in and unwrap it, do you?"

"Out of the question," I said.

"Mike. Who is it?" Mum called from the kitchen.

Perfect.

Lucy's brow wrinkled. "I thought you said your Mum was in New Zealand."

"Yep. She must have got back just now." I turned around. "Do not worry, Mum, it is no one. Stay where you are." I smiled at Lucy. "She needs to rest, what with the jet lag."

"O-*kay*," said Lucy. "Well, maybe I can open it with her now. It'll only take two minutes."

"No," I said, striding on to the doorstep and grabbing hold of the picture frame. "I will take it from here."

Lucy smiled but kept a tight grip on it. "No, Mike. I'll give it to your mum. I'd like to see what Dad drew."

I tugged it towards me but Lucy would not let go. "No, Lucy. You do not want to see this."

She pulled it towards her. Her face became determined and stern, just like before a race. "I do. Now hand it over."

"No," I snapped, a little too loudly. "Give me the flipping picture, Lucy."

"Let go of it, Mike," she said, her voice husky and serious.

This soon turned into a tug of war. She was miles stronger than me but I was not going to give up easily.[42] There was no

---

42 Yes, I am aware that she is a girl. However, she is also a girl who is able to bench press sixty kilograms. (Source: "How to Train Like a Champion" from the Preston Piranhas Swimming Club website.)

way I was going to let her see this picture. It could ruin her life.

Finally, she leaned in towards me and braced her foot against the doorstep for extra purchase. Her face was so close to mine that I could have given her an Eskimo kiss.

Over the next few seconds, six things happened:

1. The proximity of our faces caused my hands to suddenly become very sweaty.
2. Lucy gave one final yank on the picture.
3. It slipped through my greasy fingers.
4. It smashed straight into her lovely cheek.
5. She paused for a few seconds, with a strange, horrified look on her face.
6. Her cheek turned red and began to swell.

"Uh oh," I said, as she started to cry.

Chatting With Chas

Session 6 Transcript

People present and location as Session 3

Chas: So, man, tell me about Lucy King.
MS: Why?

Chas: Well, I've been reading your stuff and you said that you liked her but then you smashed her in the face and tried to spy on her. That true, bro?

MS: Yes. No. Yes. It was all accidental. I think I made that pretty clear.

Chas: All of it? Come on. Even the bit about getting into trouble for watching her getting changed? And the smack in the chops?

MS: Yes. All of it.

Chas: How did you feel about her and your brother, big guy?

MS: She can do way better than him. He is evil. He gave my hamster respiratory problems. He uses ladies' make-up. He gave me this.

[MS points at his chin.]

POM: Oooh. That looks nasty.

Chas: Yowzers. Nasty scar, man. I've got one on my leg from surfing.

[Points at leg.[43]]

Chas: I call it an Atlantic love bite.

MS: What?

Chas: Forget about it. Ain't nothing like surfing,

43 I will just mention here that, today, Chas was wearing a pair of Bermuda shorts and a vest, despite it being the middle of October. His legs were pale, weedy and wrinkly, as though they had been wrapped in wet bandages for the last fifteen years.

though. Makes me feel free. In motion with the ocean. You ever feel free?

MS: What are you talking about?

Chas: Free, you know. Like nothing is getting you down. Nothing is bothering you. You can do what you want. Ever feel like that?

[Forty-five-second pause.]

MS: No.

Chas: That's a shame, chief. A real shame. You should surf.

MS: I hate beaches.

Chas: Why's that?

[One-minute pause.]

Chas: The donkey incident again, right? Is that how you got your scar as well?

[Eighteen-second pause.]

MS: If you must know. Yes. Why do you keep going on about it?

Chas: I don't. I know I'm a crazy dude who parties at the speed of light, but my memory's OK. As I recall, it's you who's brought it up each time, man. You seem to link it to everything, you know?

[Six-second pause.]

Chas: OK. So your bro spooked the donkey. It did one. With you right there on its back. You hit the deck. Chin smash. Ouchie! Anything more you wanna give me on that? I just gotta know what the deal is.

[Twelve-second pause.]

MS: I left my inhaler in my locker. Can I go, please?

[MS exits.]

POM: I'm not sure he wants to talk about the donkey thing. He's very delicate, you know.

Chas: Yo, I dig that, but there's something funny about it. He hates his brother because of it. He hates beaches because of it. He hates donkeys because of it, for crying out loud. I mean, who hates donkeys? Wake up and smell the coffee, Patricia: this is big. We need to find out. . . Hey. Why are you smiling?

POM: You called me Patricia.

Chas: It's a cool name. And you're a cool chick. We should hang out.

POM: Oh, I'm not sure about that.

[End of transcript]

Chas

I had to escape to the library with the laptop again. Not only was the smell of beans overpowering, but he is starting to seriously get on my nerves. He is such an odd person, talking like he is some kind of breakdancer from 1988 or something. And he never shuts up about the donkey incident, as if it is a big deal. Plus, he is always leering at Miss O'Malley. I want to tell him to leave her alone and that she doesn't want anything to do with him and his disgusting, greasy ponytail and stupid clothes.

It is really strange, though. Looking at the transcripts of the sessions afterwards, I seem to be talking to him more and more. I think it is because he makes me so angry. I mean, I am trying to do what Miss O'Malley told me to do – to open up and talk more – because she is nice and I want to make her happy. I just do not want to talk to *him*. The most frustrating thing is that, however much I do not want to, I am not able to stop myself. It is like I am only giving him the answers so he will stop asking me the questions. Does that make any sense?

Probably not.

The Aftermath of the Accidental Face Smash

After giving Lucy a black eye, I ran to the kitchen and begged Mum to put on some clothes (which, surprisingly, she did). We got Lucy into the house and put some frozen peas on her face.

Luckily, in the kerfuffle, I was able to move the picture to one side.

Mum was furious.

"How could you, Michael? What is your problem?" she yelled.

"No. No," sniffed Lucy, "it was an accident."[44]

Her eye was now a really angry shade of purple.

"Well, that isn't the point," said Mum. "Michael should never have been wrestling you in the first place."

"It isn't so bad," Lucy said. "At least I'll get out of training. There's no way I'll be able to put my goggles on."

What??! I thought she *loved* training.

Suddenly she started to cry again.

"What's wrong, dear?" said Mum, putting her arm around Lucy.

"Dad will kill me for missing swimming. There's only a week till the Guild gala and the Nationals are soon after. *And* I look awful. Ste will think I'm ugly."

"Nonsense," said Mum, soothingly. "Unlike some people, Ste is not obsessed with looks." For some reason she looked at me at this point. "He is a sweet boy. And as for your father, well, I am going to see him tomorrow night and I will be happy to explain that it was all Michael's fault."

"Thanks a bunch," I said. She may as well have signed my death warrant.

---

44 I told you that she was a lovely girl.

"No. Don't do that," said Lucy. "Let me talk to him."

The front door opened and closed again. "Hey hey hey! The Stevenator is home."

Brilliant.

The Picture

Predictably, Ste threatened to kill me. Mum told him he was well within his rights to be angry. Ste said good and did this mean he could kill me? Mum genuinely seemed to be thinking this question through before Lucy said of course not and don't be silly it was just an accident and please could Ste drive her home. I mouthed a thank you at her as she left but Ste whispered in my ear that I can't go around spoiling a man's eye candy and not expect to get some beats for it. Although this did not make a great deal of sense to me, I got the message loud and clear.

After they had left I was just about to take a deep breath and relax when Mum ripped off the brown paper that covered the picture Lucy had brought round.

"Well, that is just beautiful," she cooed.

This was unfair. After everything that had just happened I was off my guard. I was not thinking straight. My reflexes were battered. My defences had been breached.

Without thinking, I glanced at the picture.

Oh my word it was horrible.

Have you ever heard the phrase "chilled to the bone"? I had always thought it was a figure of speech until that moment. I literally felt my bone marrow splintering into shards of ice.

It makes me feel quite sick to explain the picture but I will try. It was a pencil drawing in which Mum and Dad were sitting down next to each other with no clothes on. I could see everything. And I mean *everything.* In gory, gross-out, close-up detail. I thought the sight of them in the flesh was bad enough, but this was worse. It was a freeze frame; a disgusting, detailed freeze frame of possibly the worst moment in the history of mankind: The Moment My Parents Posed Nude.

For some reason, in the background, Dave had drawn a load of tanks rumbling towards them and a fighter plane crashing to Earth in a ball of flames. I guess that these were not inside Miss Skinner's classroom, but you never know. The tragedy was that Dave was, surprisingly, very good at art – a tragedy only because it made the picture even more realistic.

"I feel sick," I said.

"Don't be ridiculous," snapped Mum. "Roy. Come and look at this."

Dad walked into the room. Over the last few days he had been spending more and more time upstairs on his own. "Oh. Oh. That is. . ."

"Wonderful, isn't it?" beamed Mum. "Go and get some nails and a hammer."

Dad's mouth dropped open. "Some what and a what?"

"You heard," said Mum. "Let's get it up on the wall. Right by the front door would be perfect."

"Where?" said Dad and I at the same time.

Dad began wringing his hands together. "Look. Surely we need to discuss this. Maybe we could put it up in the spare room."

"Nonsense," said Mum. "No one will see it there."

"Exactly," ventured Dad.

Mum narrowed her eyes. "And why would we want no one to see it?"

"Er, maybe we shouldn't discuss this in front of Michael," said Dad.

"Ha," exclaimed Mum. "You're just as bad as he is. Now, listen, Roy. We agreed to do this together and we agreed to go the whole hog. This picture is going up on the wall by the front door. It is beautiful and it certainly is not something to be tucked away and ashamed of. Wasn't this the whole reason for taking our nudity outside in the first place? So we could be free, finally casting away the stupid prejudices of society."

Dad nodded sadly and skulked out to get the hammer and nails.

What a wimp.

Ste Gets His Own Back

The next night was Saturday. Mum and Dad had gone out to

see Dave King and his wife. Mum had been very excited beforehand, going on at Dad about how Dave was "going to make everything possible". I could not believe this. It was wrong for so many reasons.

1. Why would anyone want to hang around with Dave King? He is crazy. The only things he ever makes possible for me are asthma attacks.
2. What were my parents up to? I mean, the nudity was bad enough, but all this sneaking around was making me nervous. As far as I knew, they had never had any friends before, so why now, all of a sudden?
3. If they got close to Dave King, Mum would probably try to persuade him that Ste was actually nice. This could be absolutely disastrous. I was still hopeful that Lucy would find out what he was really like. Ste still had not said where he had been the evening before. In all of the confusion with Lucy's black eye, no one had even thought to ask him.

Meanwhile, the picture was up on the wall, right by the front door. At first I had thought about pulling it down or colouring it in with permanent marker but I decided that this would just get me into even more trouble. Instead, I had perfected the art of looking the other way and trying to ignore it whenever I walked past. It was an evil presence in the hallway, though, like a murderer sitting silently in the corner.

Anyway, I was upstairs in my room, wondering if I could set up a slide from my window down into the back garden. This would mean that I could avoid ever having to go past the picture.

Without warning, Ste walked in through my door. Instantly, I backed up against the wall. There was no one in the house to protect me.

"Hey hey hey, lil' bro, don't be scared," he said.

He was being nice. This is even worse than when he is being horrible.

He sat next to me on the bed. "Don't worry about yesterday. I'm prepared to accept that it was an accident, OK?"

"What do you want?" I said, cowering away from him.

"Haha. Why do you think I want something?"

I said nothing. Ste *always* wants something.

"Look," he said, "I'm prepared to forget about what you did to my girlfriend, and how you made her look ugly."[45]

"If. . ." I said.

"If you do me a little favour, that's all."

"What kind of favour?"

Ste smiled. "Well, because of you, she's grounded."

"Grounded?"

"Yeah. Grounded. She told her dad that she was messing

---

45 I told you he was horrible.

about with the picture and that the black eye was all her fault."

"Why did she do that?"

Ste laughed. "Because otherwise he would have probably pulled off your head and used it as a bowling ball."

I gulped. This seemed like quite a reasonable response. For Dave, anyway. "I do not get it. Why is *she* grounded?"

"Because," said Ste in an OK-I'll-go-slow-because-you-are-a-bit-thick sort of voice, "he was furious. Said she couldn't be going around being as stupid as this right before a big gala. Said she was jeopardizing her career. He's been mad enough with her because of me but now he's really gone nuts."

"Oh," I said. I felt really, *really* bad. "So. Why do you need me?"

Ste clapped his hands together. "Well. I'm glad you asked. . ."

Chatting With Chas

Session 7 Transcript

People present and location as Session 3[46]

Chas: Yo, man.

---

46 For some reason, today Chas was not wearing any shoes. His toes were long and thin, like an old lady's fingers. At one point he dropped his pencil and, without even looking, picked it up with his foot.

MS: Yo. I mean. Hello.

Chas: Hey. You almost spoke like a cool cat there, dude.

[Ten-second pause.]

Chas: O-kay. Where were we yesterday, my man?

MS: We were right here.

POM: Chas means. . .

MS: I know what he means. I was just. . .

Chas: Yanking my crank. Pulling my chain. I know, man. That's cool. That's cool. You're starting to make jokes. That's great. Shows we're buddies.[47] Now. We were talking about this donkey thing.

MS: [*Breathes deeply.*]

Oh. Not this again.

Chas: Sorry, man. Sorry. Some other time. Look. Tell me about your brother.

MS: What about him?

Chas: How do you get on with him now? You know, after everything.

MS: I do not.

Chas: What do you mean, you do not?

POM: Michael's brother left the country.

MS: His life was in danger. Mum paid for him to go travelling for a year. He even dropped out of sixth

---

47 Wrong.

form. He was petrified in case there were . . . further reprisals.

Chas: You mean someone was out to get him? [*Eight-second pause.*]

MS: I do not really want to talk about it right now. He is an idiot.

Chas: Do you think he deserves these . . . *reprisals*?

MS: I do not know. It *was* all his own fault, though.

Chas: Why do you feel like you dislike him so much?

MS: We have been through this.

Chas: Oh yeah, man. I get it. The hamster, the donkey, the girl. What's her name, Lucy?

MS: Please leave her out of it.

Chas: Hey, chill, man, chill. Just trying to sort out the facts.

MS: She is someone I. . .

Chas: Fancy?

MS: Admire. It is not her fault that Ste managed to hypnotize her or trick her or whatever he did to make her think he was all right.

Chas: Do you still see her?

MS: I saw her in school recently, just before a session with Miss O'Malley. We did not talk to each other. In fact, I went halfway around the school so that she did not see me. Look. I have got to get to my next lesson. Can I get out of here?

Chas: Sure, man. You go for it.

[MS exits.]

Chas: Every time he just heads off like that, big P.

POM: Big P?

Chas: It's a nickname. An affectionate one. Shows I think you're cool.

POM: Oh. [*Laughs.*]

Chas: Now. Do you wanna roll to a club on Saturday, or what?

POM: A club? No, thank you. I'm . . . erm . . . going to buy a . . . er . . . new cat.

Chas: Cool, babe. Cool. Some other time.

[End of transcript]

My Worries About Chas

I am so glad Miss O'Malley is rejecting Chas all the time. I do not think she is getting a new cat at all. Still, I cannot help worrying that, eventually, he will wear her down. She *does* seem to like him for some reason. If it was not for the time those boys poked fun of her great big hands, I think she probably would say yes to a date with him.

Ste's Plan

On that Saturday evening, when my parents were at the Kings', something unbelievable occurred. An event that would go down in history as being every bit as momentous as the first man landing on the moon, Barack Obama becoming the US president, or Lucy breaking six records in one night at last year's club championships.

Ste let me ride in his car.

OK. First he put a plastic cover on the seat. Then he told me that if I touched anything I would die. Then he made me sit with my hands on my head like a naughty three-year-old, but still, this was something special.

Apart from one tiny thing.

In the boot of the car, rattling around as we sped through red lights and overtook mobility scooters a little too closely, sat a small stepladder: Paul Beary's small stepladder, to be precise.

Ste's incredible plan was as simple as it was stupid.

1. We break into the school grounds to take Paul's ladder from its resting place behind the girls' changing room (which we had just done).
2. We drive to Lucy's house and park around the corner to avoid suspicion.
3. I help Ste to climb up to her bedroom window, then keep watch as he romances her upstairs.

4. If anyone comes along, I call out, "Freak to Love God, Freak to Love God. Abort. Abort." I have to do this in a voice "that could be mistaken for an owl". Guess whose idea this was.
5. Providing I go along with all of this and the mission passes off successfully, I will be allowed to live.

According to Ste, who was referring to himself as "The LoveGod" throughout the whole journey, "women go crazy for stuff like this". I asked him if he had ever broken into the house of a girl before whilst her psychopathic father was sitting downstairs with our mum and dad. Ste told me I was not allowed to speak in the car; I was fogging up the windows.

The Most Humiliating Thing I Have Ever Done

Ten minutes later, I was in Lucy's back garden, my heart hammering in my chest. With me standing on the top rung of the ladder and Ste standing on my head, he managed to squeeze in through the window.[48]

"Oh my word, what are you doing?" said Lucy, her beautiful voice drifting down from upstairs. "My dad will kill you."

"Relax, babe," said Ste, sounding slimy, "The Love God is here to see you."

48 I really do not think he had to kick me in the head quite so many times on the way in.

"Oh, you're terrible," she said. I hoped that she meant that he was terrible in the way that a hurricane or a serial killer or mouldy cheese is terrible. Her voice told a different story, though.

"Don't worry," said Ste. "My little bro is downstairs, kindly keeping watch."

Lucy poked her head out of the window and gave me a little wave. Her eye was massive and bright purple. She still looked nice, though.

Her head went back inside. "Has your phone been broken?" she said to him. "I can never seem to get hold of you at the moment."

"Babe, the Stevenator moves in mysterious ways," said Ste, shutting the window so that I could not hear anything else.

So there I was, alone outside the house of the girl I admired more than anyone else on Earth, standing guard to allow the man I disliked more than anyone else on Earth to spend time with her, purely to save myself from being beaten up. I had a size ten footprint on my head and it was just starting to rain. This was great. Just great.

Why Do Bad Things Only Happen to Me?

The path was pitch-black. I did not want to stand there but Ste had told me I should lurk in the shadows and stay out of sight.

The ladder was still standing just inside the back garden. There was very little sound, apart from the flapping of Dave's England flag, the pattering of the drizzle and the tiny stones from the path that I was dropping through my hands to kill time.

I was just thinking that this was pretty much the worst I had ever felt about myself when I heard the back door opening.

My whole body jolted like I was getting an electric shock. Very slowly, I peeped round the corner. Dave King was walking across the back garden with an empty bottle of wine. He stopped in front of the wheelie bins, tested its weight a few times, then began swinging it madly around his head like some kind of weapon. Luckily, he did not seem to have seen the ladder.

"Take that," he growled at an imaginary opponent. "Oh yeah, yer think you're hard? Well have one of THESE!"

I gulped with fear as he lunged forward, slicing through the air with the bottle and bringing it down on his invisible enemy's head. "How d'yer like that, eh, eh? Want some more, do yer?"

"Oh, Dave," came a voice I recognized as Mrs King's. "Just put the flipping bottle into the bin. We need to finish the meeting."

Meeting?

What did she mean, meeting? I thought Mum and Dad were going there to spend time with Lucy's parents; to hang out with them. Why would they be having a meeting?

I had to see what this was all about.

I waited until Dave dropped the bottle into the bin and went back inside.[49] Then, very slowly, I tiptoed around the corner and peered through the back window. At first the light hurt my eyes but, after a few blinks, I could make out what was going on. In the middle of the room there was a flip chart with "OPERATION FIG LEAF" written at the top of it. On the flip chart, someone had drawn a map of some sort, with arrows pointing into it from all angles. Dave came into the room, picked up a pen and started pointing at the arrows one at a time, as though he was directing a military mission.

I looked around the room. Mum and Dad were sitting on the sofa. At least twenty other people were crammed into the room, sitting on the floor and standing against the walls. Mum was intently following every word that Dave said. Dad looked extremely scared. Mrs King looked at Dave proudly. There was one other person sharing the sofa with Mum and Dad. I could not quite make out who it was until she turned her head. She had an unmistakable moustache and goss eyes.

"Miss Skinner," I whispered. What was *she* doing there? And what on Earth was "Operation Fig Leaf"?

I did not have much time to think about it because suddenly

---

49 I swear that he jabbed his finger into thin air and said, "Next time you won't have my wife here to protect you!" to his non-existent enemy. The man is seriously mad.

Dave's head jerked to the side and his eyebrows lifted up, like he was listening for something. I watched him creep slowly to the door and call upstairs.

My eyes flicked up towards Lucy's window and back to the lounge.

Time seemed to stand still. The options were simple:

1. Call up to Ste and help him to escape.
2. Run away.

Option 2 seemed the most attractive. Ste would get pummelled by Dave King and would be banned from seeing Lucy ever again. Mum would find out what Ste was really like and suddenly I would not be treated quite so badly. Also, Operation Fig Leaf, whatever it was, would end straight away. I did not like it one bit.

There was a huge problem with this plan, though. If I ran away, maybe Lucy would never forgive me. She would never speak to me or smile at me or make jokes about goggle marks with me again.

Hating myself, I cleared my throat, looked up to the window and half whispered, half shouted, in a voice that could possibly be mistaken for an owl, "Freak to Love God. Freak to Love God. . ."

Being Chased

Ste leapt out of the window. Luckily for him, I broke his fall.

"Did he see you?" I said, as we struggled to our feet.

"No," he said breathlessly, "I got out just in time. Let's go."

We charged through the gate and sprinted down the road. Despite my burning lungs, I was a good five metres in front of Ste when I heard a familiar roar from behind us. "Get back 'ere!"

"Dave!" I cried.

He let out a blood-curdling scream, then hurtled along the road behind us, gaining on us with every step. I felt like a sick antelope being chased down by a lion.

We swung around the corner, Ste's car just ahead of us.

"Slow down, slow down," panted Ste. "Take the keys and open the car."

Dave was only about thirty metres away now.

I dropped my pace slightly and held out my hands to grab the keys.

CRUNCH!

Without warning, Ste dropped his shoulder and rugby tackled me. I flew through the air, over a small wall and landed face down in someone's flower bed.

"What are you doing?" I said, spitting out a mouthful of soil. My back and face were throbbing and it felt like I had been run over.

Ste ground my face into the dirt. "It's all right, Dave. I caught him. I caught him. He won't be bothering Lucy again."

What a villain.

Ste's Version of Events

It was lucky for me that a police car just happened to be passing at the time. The officer driving it got out before Dave could actually lay a finger on me. Thankfully, he had been a little bit surprised to see two people rolling around in someone's begonias. Mum and Dad arrived a few moments later.

This is Ste's version of events, which he proudly recounted to the police officer, Mum, Dad, Miss Skinner, and Mr and Mrs King, who had followed us to see what the commotion was:

1. He had been at home, looking after me like a good brother. I had begun acting strangely, foaming at the mouth and babbling about ladders and Lucy King. He had tried to calm me down but, unfortunately, I was like a "man possessed".[50]
2. Despite his best efforts, I had sneaked out of the house. By the time he realized, it was too late. Of course, he

50 At this point, Mum nodded. *Nodded*, I tell you.

knew exactly where I was going. Not wishing to alarm Dave and his lovely wife,[51] he parked around the corner. His hope was to talk me out of whatever sick enterprise I was carrying out, thus protecting Lucy, without causing a scene or disturbing our parents' hard-earned evening of relaxation with their new friends.

3. When he arrived in the garden, he found me at the top of the stepladder, hanging half in and half out of Lucy's window, making strange noises that sounded "like a chimpanzee eating a watermelon". At that point, he heard Dave calling from inside. I fell off the ladder and ran away. Wishing justice to be done, he gave chase and bundled me over.

He finished his performance by saying that it was his deepest wish that I could be cured of my illness. He then asked if the good officer knew of any institutions where I could be locked up and given electric shock treatment to stop these impulses.

I tried to argue with him but Mum kept saying be quiet and what a big surprise and wasn't it just lucky that a fine upstanding member of the community like Ste was here to stop me.

The police asked if they could speak to Lucy but Mum cut in. "There is no need, officer. I am awfully sorry and, may I say, deeply ashamed, but this is what this boy does. Despite our best

51 Mrs King blushed when he said this.

efforts, he seems to have an unhealthy obsession with Lucy – and the naked form – and has been caught spying on her several times. Please, do not bring that poor, suffering girl into this."

"I can vouch for that," said Miss Skinner. "I caught him at school."

"An' I caught him at the swimming baths," grunted Dave.

The policeman, an enormous human being with bits of food stuck in his moustache, loomed over me. "Well, son. You do know that the maximum penalty for trespass and spying on someone is a lengthy spell in prison."

"Perhaps it's the only way to rid him of this affliction," said Ste.

"Steady on," said Dad.

Mum stood on his foot and told him to let the police do their jobs. "We've tried everything else, Roy. Perhaps all we can do now is to support him as best we can and hope that the justice system gives him a fair trial."

Had she gone completely mental?

I tried to say that I was innocent but the policeman silenced me with an aggressive sniff. Even in the dark I noticed that he had a jungle of hair sprouting out of his nostrils.

"As I say," he continued, "we do *not* take this kind of offence lightly. But on this occasion, seeing as you have such an understanding family who I am sure will deal with you properly, I am willing to let you off with a warning." He then dropped his voice and bent right down so his nose hair was almost tickling my face. "Now listen, son. I've got your name and I never, *ever* want to hear from you again. Cut. It. Out."

With each of the last three words, he jabbed me in the chest with his finger, then turned and got back into his car.

"Wait till I get you home," said Mum.

Mrs King cleared her throat and nudged Dave in the shoulder.

"Thank you for . . . er . . . helping out," mumbled Dave to my brother.

"That's OK, Mr King," said Ste. "I can only apologize for Michael's actions and will do everything I can to stop this from happening again."

Dave King looked like he was swallowing something very unpleasant. "Well, I suppose it wouldn't hurt if you were allowed round to see Lucy. Y'know, since you're 'ere."

"Hear hear," said Mum. "Michael, thank you for completely ruining our evening. Let's go home, Roy."

Chatting With Chas

Session 8 Transcript

Location and people present as Session 3

Chas: Yo, player, give me some skin.

MS: No.

POM: [*Coughs.*] Biscuit, anyone? I've got Bourbons.

MS: No, thank you. I have decided that they remind me of my brother. He is an idiot.

Chas: Word up, Miss O.M.

[Six-second pause.]

POM: I'm sorry. Does that mean you do want one or you don't?

Chas: Affirmative, babe.

POM: Right.

Chas: Yo, Michael. I think we're homeys now. Things are happening. Yesterday you really started opening up.

MS: Good grief.

Chas: So, like I say, we're getting somewhere, but I can't help but think you're not telling me everything. Now. Come on. Don't hold back, baby.

MS: What do you mean?

Chas: OK. We've talked about this donkey thing.

MS: [*Sighs.*]

Chas: We've talked about your bro. We almost talked about that babe you were in love with.

MS: Admired.

Chas: Whatever. Now we ain't never said nothing about your olds, though, and they're the big characters in this whole drama, am I right? Tell me, what is it that made you feel so bad about your parents getting their kits off? What made it so hard for you to accept it?

MS: What? Are you mad?

Chas: Let it all out, man.

MS: OK. OK. I will. These are my parents. *My parents*. And they were wandering around with nothing on. It was disgusting. End of story.

Chas: Why?

MS: Have you ever seen your parents naked?

Chas: Well, er, no.

MS: Exactly. You would not know. Would you like to see your parents naked?

Chas: Well. Different strokes for different folks.

MS: Ha. Rubbish. It is easy to sit there and say it but try eating your breakfast with a boob hanging in it. *Your own mum's boob.* Try living in your house and every time you go through the hallway there's a picture of them with *everything* hanging out staring you in the face. Try opening a door and not knowing whether you're going to see a *you-know-what* or a . . . a . . . a . . . *thingy*. Try having them flaunting their bits and pieces in public. *In public.* Is it any wonder I refuse to talk to my mum any more? Is it a massive surprise that I would rather freeze in a tent every night than have to even look at her? Is it a startling revelation to you that perhaps I might be a little bit *messed up* by everything that has happened?

POM: Are you OK, Michael? You've gone very red.

MS: [*Takes inhaler.*] I am fine. He just does not understand.

Chas: Mikey, I hold my hands up. I can't understand, buddy. But I can help you to understand.

MS: I understand perfectly, thank you.

Chas: Whatever you say, dude. But you know what? You keep letting out that rage, man. You keep letting it out. Because I think this is the key. I've said it before and I'll say it again. Freedom is what you need, man. Freedom from your own memories. Freedom from everything that's happened and everything that's holding you back. Freedom to live your life – and that, my funky pal, is why I think we're making progress. You're opening up, man, and it ain't too long before we'll be at the bottom of this whole thing. That is a wrap.

POM: Marvellous speech, Chas. Simply inspirational.

Chas: It's what I do, babe. It's what I do. Maybe I could tell you more over dinner.

MS: I'm still here, you know.

Chas: Sorry, man.

POM: Maybe another week. I've got to, erm . . . worm my new cat.

Chas: Cool.

[End of transcript]

I Cannot Stand Chas

When I left today's session, I was *furious*. Chas makes me *so* mad.

And he just will not take no for an answer from Miss O'Malley. Surely he should have got the message by now. Because of what those horrible boys did to her, she does not want anything to do with men. And that includes scrawny old skateboarders with daft clothes who live in a 1980s time warp. Therefore, he should just leave her alone. When offered the opportunity to go out with him, she would rather worm a non-existent cat. I think that says it all.

The worst thing is that, despite all this, Miss O'Malley seems to think he is a good person. If it was not for what happened at the cinema, she might even be *interested* in him. I have absolutely no idea why she *would* like him, though. Every time I see him I dislike him more.

The problem is that I go in there every time with the plan to not say anything, but then, as soon as I see him, I get so mad that I cannot stop myself. He says we are making progress but I have no idea what he means. All he does is ask me about stuff he already knows. And I wish he would stop bringing up that flipping donkey. It is getting very tiresome.

Fallout From Helping My Idiot Brother
A) The Bad Things

After what happened at Lucy's I was, predictably, in big trouble. My pocket money was stopped, and nobody at home would even acknowledge me, let alone talk to me. Well, Dad tried to, but Mum told him that I would not learn unless I was properly punished. In addition to this, I was grounded for two weeks.[52]

I had to write Dave a letter apologizing for spying on Lucy and begging to be allowed to still be a sea slug on the torchlit parade. At the start of training the next night, I had to hand it to him in one of my mum's floral envelopes. This was *so* humiliating. He read it and then scrunched it up.

"Get in the pool, you little snot rag," he grunted. "And the only reason I'll let you still be in the parade is cos my wife's already made the costumes and there's no one else with a body that's misshapen enough to fit into yours."

---

52 Of course I was allowed to go swimming. I say *allowed* but this is the wrong word. *Forced* is probably more accurate.

B) The Good Things

Well, it was more like a good *thing*. Actually, it was more a kind-of-bad-kind-of-good thing but still, when your parents are nudists and you have been grounded for spying on the girl you admire, you will take anything you can get.

When I was on my way out of the changing rooms at the end of the session, Lucy walked past me, her eye still quite badly swollen. Without saying a word, she slipped a piece of paper into my hand. I shoved it into my pocket, making sure no one saw it. When I got home, I went straight to my room and shut the door so I could look at it.

It was a letter and this is what it said (the footnotes are all mine):

Dear Michael,

Thank you so much for what you did last night. Ste told me how you forced him to rugby tackle you and then how you took the blame for the ladder and everything so that we wouldn't get found out.[53] *He even said how he tried to tell the truth to my dad but*

53 Not strictly true.

you wouldn't let him get into trouble.[54] *I can't believe you would do this for us. You are so sweet. My dad now thinks Ste is OK and, so long as he doesn't take me away from training or treat me badly, he says I can see him.*[55] *And it is all thanks to you.*

Anyway, thank you so much. You don't know how boring it was to be grounded[56] *and Ste's visit really cheered me up. It was just lucky he got out when he did.*[57] *I owe you a big hug. You are a really special friend.*

Love and kisses,
Lucy
Xxx

How Good Was That?

OK, so maybe the letter had more bad bits than good, but all that the bad bits did was tell me stuff that I already knew or had guessed anyway. Lucy loved Ste. Ste was a big fat liar. Now Dave liked Ste too.

Even so, all you have to do is count the kisses, 1-2-3. She

---

54 Not true in any way, shape or form whatsoever.
55 I really, really hope this is not true.
56 I do now.
57 Yeah. Really lucky.

owed me a big hug. I decided right there and then to cash that debt in the very next time I saw her. Oh yes. Ste was her boyfriend but she would surely find him out. I was her *special friend* and she sent me her love. Everyone knows that friends come before boyfriends. *Unlucky, Ste*, I thought. *Your reign of terror is about to end.*

This was *magnificent.*

Things Special Friends Do Together

1) Hug.
2) Kiss (three times). Not that I feel the need to kiss her, you understand.
3) Talk about how terrible one of the friend's boyfriends is and make sure they split up with each other.

Why is Happiness Always So Short-Lived?

Over the next three days, I must have read Lucy's letter about four thousand times.[58] It was all that kept me going whilst I was sitting alone in my room. I could not face going downstairs

58 The "o" and the dot above the "i" in "Love and kisses" were both hearts. Hearts, I tell you. The universal symbol for, well, good things.

much when Mum and Dad were wandering around naked, and I certainly did not want to talk to Ste. I would come home from school, collect a couple of custard creams from the kitchen, then sit on my bed until my tea was left outside the door by Mum. After eating, I would resume sitting and rereading the letter.

The only other things I could think of were:

1. What on Earth my parents had been up to at Dave King's house, what the map was for and what all of this had to do with Miss Skinner.
2. How I could get Lucy to stop going out with my brother.

I did not know at the time, but answers to both of these problems would soon turn up.

Getting Rid of Paul

On the Wednesday after I was grounded, I was walking out through the school gates with Paul Beary. As usual, he was trying to get invited round my house after school. He always had some ridiculous reason for needing to visit but I knew that all he wanted to do was catch a glimpse of Mum without her clothes on.

On this day the conversation went something like this:

Him: Hey, Mike, you'll never guess what.

Me: No. I bet I could not.

Him: You know my uncle.

Me: The one who invented the tent.

Him: Caravan.

Me: OK, yes. Uncle Caravan.

Him: Dwayne, actually. Well, anyway, guess what. Today he's going to be the first man to send a caravan into space.

Me: Space? Why on Earth would he do that?

Him: I don't know. He's bought a rocket and he's strapped the caravan to it and it's going to be fired up in about half an hour. 'S going to be amazing. You'll be able to see it from your bedroom window. Wanna watch it?

Me: Sure thing. That sounds great. Even though I am grounded I cannot think of anything I would rather do. Should we go to yours?[59]

Him: Ah, no. That's the thing. My mum's painted all of the windows in the house black so we'd only be able to watch it at your house.

Me: Your windows are black?

Him: Yep. It's because of the UFO that landed in the garden last week. These aliens got out and tried to abduct my mum but she fought them off with a hairdryer and now she thinks that if they return in their spaceship she can stop them getting

---

59 Paul does not get sarcasm.

into the house by painting the windows black because . . . hey, come back. Where are you going? Aw.

After this nonsense I went home, closing my eyes when I got to the end of the drive in preparation for meeting my parents, and entered the house as quietly as possible.

There was no reaction. The house was silent. I opened one eye, accidentally catching a glimpse of Dave's horrible drawing in my peripheral vision, then closed it and opened the other eye instead.

That was better.

"Mum? Dad? Ste?" I called, hoping they would not reply. They did not.

Excellent.

I went into the kitchen to get an apple. These days I find that I like apples more than I did before. I think that this is because their skin is thick and covers all of the flesh inside.

There was a note on the table. It said:

Michael,

Dad's taken afternoon off work. Going to meet the Kings and Miss Skinner. Not sure when we'll be home. Maybe not till v late. Food in fridge. Help self. Ste out all evening playing cricket. Remember you are grounded!

Mum

What had got into them? They had gone out. On a weeknight. To meet my crazy art teacher and my even crazier swimming coach. This was seriously suspicious. Dad had never taken so much as a moment off work before. It must have been something very important. As for Ste, well, I had never known him to play cricket.

Still. I did not give too much thought to this. For the first time in ages, I could walk around the house without fear of seeing a naked bottom or much worse staring back at me.

This was a cause for celebration. I forgot about my apple, grabbed the whole biscuit tin, then plonked myself right in front of the TV.[60] Shoving a custard cream into my mouth, I settled down to some mid-afternoon quiz shows. I like these shows because they are not silly like children's TV shows; and they are not all about surfers called Brad and their girlfriends called Briony who turn out to be their long-lost sisters like in those stupid Australian soap operas that are on after school.

After about an hour and nine biscuits, the phone rang. I did not want to answer it because I was trying to figure out the anagram that comes up at the end of my favourite quiz show. Still, it rang and it rang for ages, so I felt like I had to. Maybe it was Mum, making sure I had not gone out.

---

60 I had taken to sitting on the carpet as I now realized that both of the armchairs and the sofa had been sat on for the last eight years by my parents' bare bums.

I picked up the phone. "Hello."

"Oh, hi. Is that Mike?" A lovely soft voice. It could only be. . .

"Lucy. Hi. How are you? Stalker."

"What?"

"Oh, sorry. Sorry. It's the anagram. On the telly. My programme has just finished."

"Oh. Ha ha. I was watching that too. You're very clever. I can never get them."

"Thank you. How are you? How is your eye?"

"Better, thanks. Still hurts when I wear goggles, but like Dad says: 'No pain, no medals'."

"You owe me that hug, remember."

"What? Oh yeah, of course. Listen, thanks for that. You're amazing."

"I know, thank you." A little bit cocky but who cares? I was on a roll and *amazing* people are allowed to be a bit cocky.

"Is Ste there?"

Talk about wrecking the mood.

"He is playing cricket." My teeth gritted together.

"Cricket. Oh. I didn't know he played. That's . . . unusual. I mean, it's just he never. . . Well, he said he'd come round tonight cos it's my only evening off from training this week and. . . Well. Erm. Could you get him to call me?"

"Sure."

Not a chance.

What *was* he up to, anyway? This was not the first time he had disappeared with some lie. Do you know what? Lucy and I were friends. *Special* friends. And what kind of special friend would not try to protect *their* special friend from a nasty person. The time to sow the seeds of doubt had arrived.

"Well, actually," I said, in as casual a voice as I could manage, "now I think about it, I have *never* known him to play cricket before. And I guess that he has been acting a little strange—"

"Oh my God!" Lucy yelped.

"What is it?"

"The TV. It's. . ."

I turned to look at the TV in the lounge. I froze. The phone dropped out of my hand.

Things had just reached a whole new level of horror.

The Absolute Worst Moment of My Entire Life Part IV

The local news was now on the TV. The screen panned across the Flag Market in Preston, the main square in the centre of the city. A crowd of people were standing around in a large circle. Some were laughing, some were cringing with embarrassment and some were filming with their mobile phones. All of them were looking at the same thing.

In front of the library, about thirty people were draped across benches and the flagstones. All of them were. . .

". . .naked and proudly displaying their bodies to amazed shoppers," declared the reporter in a ha-ha-ha-isn't-this-a-jolly-good-laugh voice. "Onlookers described how the nudists appeared from all sides of the square as though it were a 'military operation'. Police soon arrived, but the exhibitionists escaped without a single arrest being made."

The picture showed the nudists scattering as a group of policemen in luminous jackets poured into the square. A naked woman whose body was (thankfully) blurred out ran straight up to the camera.

"They can arrest us if they want, but we'll always be free. Free to be ourselves. Free to be naked. Free from society's shackles. Free! Free! Free, I tell you! This is only the beginning. We want to be naked all of the time. Try and stop us!" she screamed, her eyes crazed and flecks of spit flying from her mouth on to the lens. As a policeman ran towards her, the woman sprinted away and disappeared up a side street.

That woman was my mother.

What Miss Skinner Had to Do With All This

As I staggered back against the wall, Miss Skinner appeared

onscreen with the words "local artist" underneath her.

"I helped to organize the whole thing," she said proudly.

"And what was it all about?" asked the reporter.

Miss Skinner grinned, her eyes whirling around in different directions. "Freedom."

Not that flipping word again.

She rubbed her hands together. "It was about taking on the law, fighting for our rights. And it was about art, my dear girl. Art. This was the first time that Preston has been witness to M.A.N."

"M.A.N.?"

"Mass Artistic Nudity. I captured the whole thing on my camera. It will be a beautiful picture that challenges society's blinkered views of the world. I mean, why should people wear clothes in public?[61] Operation Fig Leaf was a huge success."

At that point, the front door opened.

What Operation Fig Leaf Was All About

Mum burst into the front room. "Haha. What a day. What a victory for freedom."

I slowly turned my head towards her. "I saw you on television."

---

61 I could have given her a long list of reasons.

To my surprise, this made Mum's smile grow so wide that the tendons in her neck stuck out. She looked like a chicken straining to lay an egg. "We made it on to the TV? How wonderful."

The local news had now moved on to a story about a skateboarding kitten.

I swallowed down the sour taste of sick. "What on Earth were you doing? You were in public. There were people everywhere."

Mum picked up the phone off the floor, hung it up, then clapped her hands together. "I know. I know. Wasn't it amazing? Oh, Dave King and Miss Skinner are just genius. *Genius.* It was like a mil—"

"—itary operation, I know," I said, getting angry.[62] "But I asked you already, what on Earth were you doing?"

Mum leaned back on the sofa. She was wearing all-black clothes. "Not that I have to explain myself to *you* but, for your information, *that* was Operation Fig Leaf."

"I know," I said, remembering the people looking at the map with the arrows all over it in Lucy's front room.

Mum's eyes seemed to lose focus, as though she were reliving the whole thing. "Oh, it was wonderful. Artistic expression at its best."

"*Artistic?*" I cried. "There's nothing artistic about sitting in

---

62 A) For the obvious reason. B) Because I realized that Mum had just hung up on Lucy.

the nude with a whole bunch of shoppers gawping at you."

Mum tutted. "Art is all about challenging people, Michael. It is all about making people think and then changing the way they think and then. . ."

At that point, Dad walked in sheepishly, raised a weak smile at me, then hurried straight upstairs.

"Is he happy about all of this?" I said.

Mum rolled her eyes. "Oh, your father couldn't manage it. He said it was too cold. He stayed in the car." Her voice was dripping with contempt.

"I just do not understand why you have to keep *doing* things like this all of the time. I do not even know you any more," I said, feeling my throat begin to tighten.

"Oh, Mikey," said Mum. She went to put her hand on my shoulder, but I shrugged her away. "Look. You have to understand that I am still your mum, but things have, well, changed a bit. The time you saw us in the lounge, it opened a door for me. It meant I didn't have to hide this any more. It made me realize that the whole law that you have to wear clothes is stupid and pointless. It made me realize that you can't be free unless you act the way you want."

"But what if acting the way you want makes me feel bad?" I said, tears stinging my eyes. "I have got to go to school. People will. . ."

"Oh, let them, Michael. Let them talk. Who cares? What matters is living your life the way you want to."

"But I *cannot* live my life the way *I* want to, can I? Not with you prancing round without your pants on. Why did you have to drag Dave King into it? What about poor Lucy?"

Mum rolled her eyes. "Oh yes, and you really cared about her feelings when you were spying on her, didn't you? You don't know the first thing about Dave King or his family."

I stormed out of the front room and through the front door. On my drive I bumped straight into Paul Beary.

"Oh great," I said. "What do you want?"

Chatting With Chas

Session 9 Transcript

People present and location as Session 3

Chas: Yo, rude dog.

MS: [*Shakes head.*] Hello.

Chas: So what's happening, bro?

MS: You are not my *bro*. You would not want to be my *bro*. I do not like my *bro*.

Chas: I dig. I dig. So we were talking about freedom. How we need you to open up. To be free from all the crazy rubbish that's in your head and holding you back. What do you think about freedom, my man?

MS: [*Takes a deep breath.*] Freedom is stupid.

Chas: What? Are you serious, man? Stupid? Woah. You are out of whack. You can't think that.

[Fifteen-second pause.]

MS: I can think that. I do not want to be "free", as you call it, because what you mean by free is to be able to run around and do whatever you like and not care about rules or other people or routines or anything else. Well, I *like* rules. I *like* to be on time for things. I *like* to be normal and dependable. I *like* to have a routine to follow.

Chas: Are you messing with me?

MS: No. There are three groups of people: those who are *not* free, those who *are* free and those who *think* they are free. All the best people I know are not free. Take Lucy, for example, and how she had to train all the time even though she did not like it. She is not free. And Miss O'Malley. She is not free either. She has her whole worry about the Irish boy with the gloves.

Chas: The what?

POM: Forget about it.

[Three-second pause.]

Chas: OK. Maybe some other time. Well, little dude. You're seriously opening up. Miss O'Malley, this kid is something special.

POM: I knew he had it in him. Squash, anyone?

Chas: Righteous, babe. Still, Michael. I don't agree. Just cos I'm free it don't necessarily hurt anybody else. You'll have to prove me wrong. Explain what you mean.

MS: People who want to be "free" in the way that you mean it are usually making someone else suffer. They let people down. They stop other people from living the way *they* want to live. My mum with her nudity. My brother with the way *he* was with Lucy. You cannot have this stupid freedom thing without other people getting hurt. It is not possible.

Chas: Oh, awesome, my man. We have hit the jackpot here. I can really see what makes you tick – yo, thanks for the squash, Big P – and I get exactly what you're saying. But I still don't agree. Take me, for example. I feel free. I party every day. I live like a crazy dog. But you know what? I make sure that Chas never lets anyone down. I got it tattooed across my shoulders in Arabic: "Never hurt no one." It's like a motto. So tell me. What am *I* doing wrong?

[Eighteen-second pause.]

MS: Do you really want to know?

Chas: Yeah, man. I'm a big boy. I can handle it.

[Five-second pause.]

MS: OK. Do not blame me. You are part of the other group.

Chas: The other group? What other group?

MS: The group that *thinks* they are free but they are not. I mean, why do you speak like that?

Chas: Like what?

MS: Like you are some kind of New York breakdancer from about a million years ago. I do not like to be rude but you are quite old.

Chas: Old?

MS: Yes. I reckon that your ponytail is at least sixty per cent grey. There are wrinkles around your eyes and the skin on your arms is starting to sag. I notice these things. I think that this tells me you are a little bit old.

[Thirty-second pause.]

Chas: What do you mean old? Old like your big brother.

MS: [*Laughs.*]

[One-minute pause.]

Chas: Old like your mum and dad?

MS: No. Absolutely not. They are both forty-two. My mum is forty-three next month. You have to be at least seven years older than them.

[Two-minute pause.]

MS: Look. I am sorry I noticed your age.

Chas: Mikey, it's no probs. I'm totally down with what you're saying.

MS: You think that by dressing like this and speaking like this you are free. But you know what? I wonder why a fifty-year-old. . .

Chas: Forty-nine.

MS: Forty-nine-year-old man dresses like some kind of graffiti artist's granddad. I mean, you try to *act* like you are free and easy and cool but it cannot be natural, can it? You cannot really be free. You are obviously controlled by wanting to be young again.

[Twelve-second pause.]

Chas: This is the way I am. . .

[Five-second pause.]

Chas: . . .dude.

MS: Is it? Is it really? I mean, look, there is no need to cry.

Chas: I ain't crying. Carry on, man. I've got an ulcer in my tear gland. Had it since I was a kid. Sometimes it leaks, that's all. It's no biggy.

MS: OK, well. You are trying so hard to *pretend* to be yourself that you end up being someone else. I mean, I would like you a lot more if you just acted your age.

Chas: You would?

[Ten-second pause.]

Chas: You would?

MS: Sure.

[Thirty-second pause. POM hands Chas a tissue and pats him on the back.]

POM: Let's stop this recording. Whoops. No. Wrong button. Damn these massive fingers. Michael, can you press stop for me?

[End of transcript]

Feeling Bad for Chas

After the recording stopped, Miss O'Malley started hugging Chas and patting his back and he was making a noise like a sick wallaby that had been left out in the rain. I could barely make out what he was saying, but it was something about always trying to make people like him but they never did and instead he just spent every evening alone eating baked beans on toast.[63]

As quietly as I could, I slipped out of the room and came straight here to the library with my laptop. I did not mean to make him upset. He just asked what I thought and I told him.

---

63 Hence the overpowering smell, I suppose.

This made me feel pretty bad. He may be an idiot but I guess he has never tried to hurt anyone.

I do not even know where that whole speech came from. It is not like I had rehearsed it or even thought too much about it. The thing was that it all seemed to make sense when I was saying it. I *do* think that all this freedom stuff that Mum always went on about is a load of rubbish. And I *do* think that Chas tries too hard to be someone else. I just do not know what all this has to do with me.

I am going to continue with my story now before I make myself depressed.

Paul Beary Sniffing Around

When I left off last time, Paul Beary was standing on my drive and I had just asked him what he wanted.

"Can I come in?" he said.

"No," I snapped, "you cannot. I know why you are here and you can just forget about it. She is wearing clothes now anyway."

"But, Mike. . ."

"Oh, what? You want to come in so you can watch your uncle fire his caravan into space. You must think I am stupid."

I pushed past him. As I was turning out of the drive, he said, "It's about Lucy."

Straight away, I turned around. "What about her?"

Why I Am Lucky to Have a Friend Like Paul

A short version of Paul's story:

1) After I had left him at the school gates, he had remembered that it was Wednesday and that this was a perfect time to watch the Year 10 girls' hockey team getting undressed.
2) On arriving at the place where his ladder usually was, he found that it was not there. Disappointed, he decided to go home and email his French girlfriend.[64]
3) He took a short cut across the park. As he was walking along, he saw my brother sitting on a bench by the swings, snogging a girl.

"I knew it was him because I was really close to them," he said.

This made me feel a little uneasy. "Exactly how close?"

Paul shoved his big fat face forward so it was about a centimetre away from mine. "About this close. They were really into each other. I stayed there for ages until she noticed me and turned around. I had to leg it before he caught me."

---

64 I know. I had to not laugh at this point as it would have ruined the story.

I took a step back. "How long were you standing there for, Paul?"

"Oh I dunno. About. . ." He took a deep breath. "Eight or nine minutes."

"Eight or nine minutes?! You are seriously messed up. I am surprised Lucy did not smack you in the face."

Paul's face dropped. "That's the thing. The girl wasn't Lucy."

Everything Falls Into Place

I had forgotten about Ste's supposed cricket match and Lucy ringing up but now it all made sense. All of the times when he said he was playing football or poker or whatever, he was with some other girl.

The *rogue*.

How could he do that to her? How could he do it to Lucy King: top-notch swimmer, all-round lovely person and my *special friend*, for heaven's sake.

At the same time, I could not help thinking that maybe this was *not* such a bad thing. I mean, it would obviously be in Lucy's best interests if she were to find out. . .

"You know," I said, "it is a shame you did not collect any evidence."

Paul looked a bit sheepish. "*Ahem*. Yeah."

"Hang on," I said, as he suddenly found his shoelaces very

interesting, "does that mean you *did* collect evidence?"

Paul scratched his face with his chubby fingers. "Shame not to. What with mobile phone technology being the way it is and all that."

Of course! This was *Paul Beary* I was talking to!

"Hang on. You filmed it. You filmed it on your phone. You are something else, you know that? You are disgusting, sick . . . and . . . and . . . and brilliant!"

Paul's eyebrows shot up. "What?"

"Part of me is a bit freaked out, of course, Paul. I mean, you really need to sort this out. But this is superb. This is just what I need. All we have got to do is show Lucy."

"But your brother will kill me. He's bound to know it was me."

"Did he see you?"

"I don't know. I legged it as soon as the girl started to turn around. Maybe I got round the corner before he saw who I was, but still. . ."

It was too late. I was already devising my plan.

The Plan

The plan was as follows:

1. Paul would be standing somewhere, pretending to struggle with his mobile phone.

2. When Lucy came past, he would ask her if she knew how to play videos on it as he had just been texted one from a mystery number.
3. Being nice, she would help him and, therefore, watch my brother snogging another girl.
4. Lucy would dump Ste.
5. As Lucy's special friend, I would be there to help her pick up the pieces.

Paul did not want to take part but I told him that he had to. If he did not do it, I would be forced to tell Ste exactly who owned the big fat bum that he saw retreating across the park shortly after the girl he was snogging suddenly unlocked her lips from his and screamed.

All we needed was a place and time that Paul would be guaranteed to find Lucy. There were two options:

A) Outside the leisure centre on Saturday at 1:50 p.m.
B) Between the gym and swimming changing rooms at the leisure centre on Friday night at 8 p.m.[65]

I did not want to do option A) for a very good reason: this was the time when she would be going in to the leisure centre for

---

65 Every Friday Lucy does one hour in the gym followed by one hour in the pool. OK, so I have written down her training schedule in an old exercise book. What is wrong with understanding how elite athletes work?

the Guild gala. One-fifty p.m. would be just ten minutes before the opening ceremony, when the team from our French twin town would be led along the poolside by their mayor. As Lucy would be competing in this high-profile international competition in all four strokes, plus the individual medley and two relays,[66] I guessed that she would be too focused to stop and talk to some obese kid with a broken phone.

"Hey," said Paul, "I've told you, I'm just big boned."

"Sorry," I said, realizing that I had been thinking aloud. "Just make sure you are there. Remember, the plan will only work if you make out that you have no idea what is on the film. Otherwise Ste will find out and you will be dead."

"Don't worry," said Paul, "my mum was in the SAS. She's given me loads of training for this sort of thing."

How the Plan Worked . . . or Did Not

Normally I do not train on a Friday. It is Elite Squad swimmers only. On this evening, though, I wanted to be there to make sure Paul did not mess up. At five to eight, I hid behind a large plant in the foyer of the leisure centre. It was the first time I had ever done something like this. Paul loitered outside the girls'

---

66 Source: Preston Piranhas Swimming Club website ("Piranha Amongst the Frogs" – article all about Lucy's preparation for the gala).

changing rooms. It was definitely not the first time he had done something like *that*.

At eight p.m. on the dot, Lucy came out of the gym, red-faced and swigging from an energy drink bottle. Her eye was now black, her hair was matted with sweat and her walk had a kind of exhausted stagger to it.

She looked lovely.

I stayed crouched in my hiding place, completely out of sight.

"Hi, Mike," she said as she walked past. "What are you doing behind the plant?"

Perfect. I stood up slowly. "Oh. You know . . . just . . . seeing how well it's growing."

"Growing. Right," she said, squinting at the plant. "I'm not sure but I think that's a plastic plant. Anyone would think you were spying on me."

The last bit was meant as a joke, I think, so I laughed. In fact, I laughed so hard that Lucy gave me a really puzzled look and took a few steps backwards.

I had to do something fast.

"Oh wow," I said, pointing at Paul, "look at that fat idiot over there. He cannot even work his mobile phone."

Lucy looked over at Paul. He did not even have the phone out of his pocket at this point. This was a disaster.

"Mike, what are you talking about?" said Lucy.

Paul stopped gawping at the elite female swimmers who were walking into the changing rooms and suddenly pulled out his mobile phone. "OH NO!" he bellowed. "THIS MOBILE PHONE WON'T WORK. IF ONLY SOMEONE WOULD HELP ME TO WATCH A VIDEO ON IT THAT I HAVE BEEN SENT BY AN ANONYMOUS PERSON WHO I HAVE NEVER EVER MET. I REALLY NEED TO WATCH IT THIS MINUTE EVEN THOUGH I HAVE NO IDEA WHAT IT IS A VIDEO OF."

"What's going on, Mike?" asked Lucy, her voice barely calm. "And what is *he* doing here? I thought he was banned from the leisure centre after the scuba-diving incident."

I gulped. "Well, Lucy, I did not want to be the one who told you, but. . ."

Lucy Takes the News Rather Well

After I explained what had happened, Lucy snatched the phone off Paul. The aggression she showed in doing this surprised me a lot. She watched the video with her lips pursed together. By the time it reached the end bit (when the picture jolts up and down and there is a loud noise of heavy breathing as Paul runs away), her teeth were gritted in anger and the pink flush had drained from her face. She still looked lovely.

"Sorry we had to show you. . ." I said.

Lucy took a deep breath. "I suppose I had to see it. I think I'm going to. . ."

With that, she suddenly dropped her bag and sprinted off, taking the phone with her.

"Where's she going? She's got my phone," said Paul.

I knew exactly where she was going. And I knew exactly who she was going to see.

"We are dead," I murmured. I had to get to my house before she did.

Ste Gets His Comeuppance

After pelting it home on my bike, I burst in through the front door. Ste's bedroom light was on. Maybe I could warn him or get him out of the house or do something before Lucy arrived.

As I bounded up the stairs, Mum yelped up after me: "Don't you be disturbing Ste and Lucy."

Unbelievable. She had made it here before me. I suppose there was no chance of me beating an elite athlete in a race, even when I was cycling and she was on foot. Perhaps I should not have wasted time putting on my reflective jacket and checking that my lights were working.

Ste's room is right next to mine. I grabbed a glass from my bedside table and held it up to the wall, pressing my ear against the bottom of it. I could hear Lucy's echoey voice. She sounded like she was crying.

". . .and look – you can even see that it's your face, Ste. It's *definitely* you."

"Look, baby. . ."

"Don't you *baby* me."

"OK. Look, Lucy, I don't know what to say. That was from ages ago. Before I met you."

"Yeah? Well, where were you the other night when you were meant to be playing cricket? Or the time when you were at the cinema *with your friends*? Or when you were playing football? Or on your poker night? I just don't think I can trust you. You know that you're all I've got outside of swimming. I *hate* swimming. I hate it so much and you were the only thing that got me through the last few weeks and now this."

I felt *really* bad.

Suddenly Ste's door opened. There was a flurry of feet down the stairs, and then the front door slammed shut.

A few moments later my door opened. It was Ste and his face was murderous.

"Thanks a lot, bum-wad. You've gone and got the Stevenator dumped. The Stevenator never gets dumped."

I backed up against the wall. "Well, yeah, but you shouldn't have. . ."

"Shut it, you little freakazoid. I'll get her back, don't you worry. They always come crawling back. But just remember this one thing. You've got a big gala tomorrow."

"So?"

"You've got to sleep sometime."

He gave me a sinister smile and stroked his horrible little goatee. Then he walked out.

Chatting With Chas

Session 10 Transcript

People present and location as Session 3

Chas: Good morning, Michael.

[Eighteen-second pause.]

MS: Hello. You look. Different.[67]

Chas: Yes. Maybe . . . well, maybe you kind of got me to realize something last time.

POM: I think he looks lovely.

Chas: Thank you, Miss O'Malley.

MS: I especially like the beard and the ponytail.

Chas: But I got rid of both of them.

---

67 I was amazed when I saw Chas this morning. He was dressed, well, *almost* like a normal person. OK, he was still wearing basketball trainers, but his jeans were no longer so tight they looked like a second skin. His T-shirt was plain white (only slightly stained) and he was wearing a suit jacket. A *suit jacket*, I tell you. The smell of beans was almost entirely absent as well.

MS: Exactly.

[Five-second pause.]

Chas: Ha ha. Very good.

[Ten-second pause.]

MS: I am sorry for making you upset last time. I did not mean to. I just felt like—

Chas: Nonsense, Michael. You were right. I was trying. . .

[Three-second pause.]

MS: Too hard?

Chas: No. Well. Yes. But . . . look. I work with young dudes – sorry, *people* – like you all the time. I am always trying to . . . get down with them. Get to their level, get inside their heads, you dig? I mean, you understand?

MS: Perfectly.

Chas: Maybe it just wasn't the right way to do it. You just showed me I needed to be less. . .

[Three-second pause.]

MS: Strange?

Chas: False. I mean, I can still party at the speed of light, right? I've just got to be professional as well. Maybe act my age a bit more. There comes a day when you've just got to hang up your skateboard for good. Isn't that right, Miss O.M.? When you get to our age you've got to wake up and smell the coffee –

you can't keep trying to be eighteen.

POM: *Our* age? I think that I'm a few years younger than you.

MS: Yes. I would estimate at least nineteen years younger. The first time I met you, Chas, I thought you were Miss O'Malley's dad.

Chas: That's quite. . .

[Thirteen-second pause.]

[MS and POM both laugh.]

POM: Oh, Michael. You are wicked.

MS: I am simply, how would you say it? Er . . . yanking your crank, Chas. In actual fact, you only look about eight years older than Miss O'Malley.

Chas: Thank you very much. I think. Well. I suppose I'm glad you've cheered up. I take it things have improved at home.

[Five-second pause.]

MS: Things are *better*, I suppose, considering. I have made a compromise. I am still living in the tent but now I have put it up in my room instead of the garden. It was becoming frightfully cold out there. I mean, it *is* October and I am very susceptible to getting chills.

Chas: [*Chuckles.*] Well, I guess that is a start. And your family?

MS: I spoke to Mum the other day for the first

time since the torchlit procession and it was OK. I mean, all I did was ask her where my thermal vest was, but we did not have an argument at least. The police have dropped the case against her now so she will not be going to prison. This is a good thing.

Chas: Yes. Yes, it is. Michael, I am very happy. I think that, finally, you're beginning to surf with the tide, so to speak. I'm going to ask you something which you may well not like, but I think it is very important. And I think that now is the right time to ask.

MS: What is it?

POM: It really isn't so bad.

Chas: I think you have made great progress. I think you're nearly there. Things seem to be thawing out at home. But I still think that, for you to be happy in yourself, you need to get to the bottom of what it was that made you hate the whole nudity thing so much. What it was that made you feel so trapped. What it was that made you hate your brother so much. Why you are so bothered about people looking at you. Why you are obsessed with order and control. You get me?

MS: Yes, I suppose so.

Chas: I still think it has something to with that

whole donkey incident. . . No, Michael, I know you don't want to talk about it, but that is why I think it is so important. We need to make you free from this. Now, I know how you feel about "freedom", but it is my professional opinion that you are a slave to something that has happened in your past. You act the way you do because of something bad that happened a long time ago.

MS: Right.

Chas: So I want to try some regression therapy.

MS: Re-what?

Chas: I help you to relax and then we go back through your memories and replay the one we want in your head, like choosing an old film, then watching it. It will be useful in finding out exactly why this one memory causes you so much pain. From there, you will hopefully be able to resolve your problems.

MS: You are going to hypnotize me?

Chas: Er. Well. I might not call it that but, well, yes.

MS: OK.

Chas: You mean you'll do it. I must say I am surprised.

MS: So am I.

Chas: Great. Well, we'll do it tomorrow.

POM: Oh, well done, Michael. And well done, Chas. You were outstanding.

[End of transcript]

What Did I Just Agree To?

I have just got home and I still cannot figure out why I just said I would let him hypnotize me. What was I thinking? It must have been because I was shocked by his appearance and the fact that he did not call me "babe" or "big dude" even once. I found him a lot nicer than before and I definitely prefer the way he is now: not trying to act like a kid the whole time. I like him better as himself. In fact, I do not even think he is that much of an idiot any more.

Still, I am not looking forward to being put in a trance.

The Morning of the Guild Gala

The night after Ste threatened me, I tried to stay awake but eventually I must have dozed off. I woke up on the Saturday morning, face down on my bed feeling groggy. I quickly checked around my room at the stuff that Ste was most likely to have stolen or damaged: my bank card (still hidden in my briefcase), my scrapbook of newspaper cuttings about Lucy (so what, I have a collection – she is in the paper a lot and, when you admire someone as much as I do, you are perfectly willing to go to the library now and again to search through local newspaper archives to find any old articles about them you may have missed) and my secret cache of custard creams. He had not touched any of them. This made me feel relieved. In the bathroom, I checked my eyebrows and my hair (neither of which had been shaved off) and then went downstairs. Mum and Ste were in the dining room having breakfast. Of course, Mum was not wearing anything. I tried to ignore this blood-curdling fact.

"Hey hey hey, sleepyhead," said Ste. "How are you doing? Just a few hours till the big gala. Are you nervous, little fella?"

I did not like this. It is never good when Ste is nice to me.

"I thought you were angry," I said, sliding into a chair and pouring a bowl of cornflakes.

"Not me," Ste smiled.

"Not having Coco Pops, Michael?" said Mum.

"Definitely not," I replied, shivering.

"New day, new life, Mikey boy," said Ste. "Sorry the Stevenator got a bit funny last night. I was just . . . cranky. I'll speak to Lucy after the gala and straighten it all out."

"Oh, you two aren't having problems, are you?" said Mum. I still had not looked at her.

Ste smiled. "No, no. Fear not, Ma. Poor Lucy's just a bit uptight before all her races today. Beach-ball Paul wound her up yesterday with some stupid prank and she got upset when she was telling me about it. Understandable, really. She just needed to let off steam so she can focus on the gala, but she'll be absolutely fine. I don't mind her venting at me – as long as it helps her get her head straight before her races."

"Oh, she is such a lovely girl, Ste. You two deserve each other."

I nearly choked on my cornflakes.

Ste downed his orange juice and stood up. "Anyway. The Stevenator is going out to get Lucy a present for winning everything today. Mikey. You do your best and just let me know how you get on, OK. I'll be very keen to find out."

I did not like the way he winked at me on the way out. Earlier, I wrote about what winks might mean. This was definitely the kind of wink that a baddie in a film does to let his victim know that he has a secret, evil plan.

The Guild Gala

At one p.m. that day, I was sitting on the poolside at the swimming baths, shivering under my dressing gown. The balcony was packed. Somewhere in the crowd was Mum. I had not looked up at her but, thankfully, I knew that she was wearing clothes. On the way in, a few people had nudged each other and muttered something about her. Unfortunately, her fame was growing fast, and for all the wrong reasons.

All along the poolside were swimmers from every age group of our club. I searched and searched everywhere for Lucy but I could not see her.

At three minutes past one, there was a fanfare and a very French-looking man with a big gold chain round his neck strolled on to the poolside.[68] I guessed he was the mayor of Preston's twin town. Behind him streamed a long line of French swimmers, who waved to the balcony as they were cheered by all of the mums and dads.

Preston's mayor went up to his French counterpart and shook hands with him. They exchanged flags and posed for pictures, and then our mayor got hold of a microphone. He then made a long speech. The main points were:

1. The Preston Guild (as previously mentioned, this is something to do with having the right to hold a market in the city) is a big deal. Apparently.
2. We welcome our friends from France to this sporting contest.

---

68 I do not know what in particular about him looked French. I mean, he was not riding a bicycle or carrying onions around his neck. He just *did*, that is all.

3. We are all looking forward to seeing some great swimming.

The speech could have been fifteen seconds long but ended up lasting for twelve minutes. Afterwards, he posed for some pictures, and then the French mayor declared "zegala" open.

I have not appeared in many galas as I do not usually get picked for the team. However, I have been in a few club championships because everyone in the club has to enter these (even people who fall off the blocks before their race). Anyway, if there is one thing I know about galas, it is that they are boring. People dive in. They swim up and down. Someone wins. Everyone else does not. Then we have the next race. Repeat for four hours.

I was only in one race. This was the junior gents' 50m freestyle. I was not in this race because I am good at freestyle; just because I am less bad at it than the other strokes. The programme of events said that this was well down the list, immediately after Lucy's first race. By race three my backside was already numb and I was seriously fed up.

After about an hour and a half, I sat up with a start. The announcer called for the competitors in the ladies' open age group 50m butterfly to make their way to the starting place.

This was Lucy's first race.

I scanned around for her. Brutus the Beefcake and a couple of French girls lined up behind the blocks, slipped off their dressing gowns, adjusted their goggles and began shaking out their arms and legs, raising a hand as their names were announced.

"And in lane four," said the announcer, "Lucy King."

Silence. She was not there.

"Lucy King," he repeated.

Dave King was prowling up and down the poolside. He whispered something in the ear of the announcer, who said, "Could Lucy King please make her way to the starting blocks?"

The sound of a lot of people talking at once buzzed around the poolside. She was not here. Lucy King, the pride of Preston Piranhas Swimming Club, had not turned up. I gulped. This was not good.

The announcer repeated himself. Dave snapped his pen in half. The chattering got louder.

And then Lucy emerged from the changing rooms. My heart fluttered. The chattering turned to applause.

Lucy did not respond.

She walked straight past all the swimmers without looking at them. Her face was white with red splotches and the bags under her eyes were so dark that you could barely tell which one had been hit with the picture frame. Her cap was half on and she was dragging her dressing gown behind her.

She. Looked. Awful.

I never thought I would write that, but she did. She looked like she had not slept all night and she had been crying non-stop. Her dad tried to say something to her but she ignored him and got straight on to her block, absent-mindedly dropping her gown on the floor.

"On your marks. . ."

The swimmers tensed up on the blocks.

"Bang!"

They dived in, slicing through the water and emerging again after ten metres. Arms barely causing a splash, they powered down the first length. At the turn Lucy was half a stroke ahead of the others. From her push-off, her legs gracefully drove her into a two-metre lead.

"Go on, Lucy!" I cried, as the noise in the pool rose to fever pitch.

Then something strange happened.

On her second stroke off the wall, she took a glance behind her on both sides. This is not as easy as it sounds. Also, even I know that it is not a good idea because it wastes time. It gave the others a tiny chance to claw back at her. On her next stroke, she did the same. What was she thinking? This was mental.[69]

I quickly glanced at Dave. His eyes were bulging out like a chameleon and he was screaming so loudly I thought the vein in his neck might burst.

---

69 Lucy's top tip for winning a race is to focus on the wall and nothing else. Do not worry about the other swimmers. If you lose focus on your goal, you will waste time and this "turns gold into mould". Source: Preston Piranhas Swimming Club website: "Winning the Easy Way".

The other four swimmers were now level with Lucy. Suddenly the way that she was swimming changed. On her next stroke, she lazily flopped her arms forward, as though she was giving up. She did not even bother to bring her arms out of the water for the next one. By now, she was three metres behind the other girls, slowly kicking her legs with her face under the water and her arms dragging along by her side.

She was *trying* to lose.

At the end of the pool, Brutus the Beefcake was waving her fist in the air in victory. The two French girls had pretty much tied in second and third. Way behind them, Lucy drifted to the end in last place.

Dave King's mouth was open in a great big O. As Lucy pulled herself out of the water, his hand dropped to his side and his clipboard fell to the floor. Without looking at him, she scurried off down the poolside and into the changing rooms. Her hand was over her eyes and she was crying.

The parents on the balcony were chattering so loudly that the announcer had to repeat himself three times: "Junior gents' fifty metres freestyle. Swimmers to their blocks, please."

I sat up with a start.

My head was all over the place as I made my way to the blocks. How could I be ready to swim? How could the gala still be going ahead? The best swimmer in the club had just given up in a race and stormed off in tears. This was the worst moment in the history of the club; maybe in the history of swimming.

My Race, Not That I Played Much of a Part In It

When I reached the end I had a look at the other boys. There was one of the elite swimmers from our club and two towering French boys, both of whom had sideburns and looked about twenty-six years old. I gulped. Last place again. How grimly predictable.

The announcer said the name of the other three swimmers and each one got a round of applause. Then he said my name. As I have mentioned earlier, I do not like to be looked at. As a result, with all of these people watching, I preferred to keep my dressing gown on until the absolute last moment.

I waved to the balcony.[70] Then, with a deep breath, I slipped off my dressing gown.

Have you ever heard a vacuum cleaner being switched on? As soon as you press the "on" button it makes a sudden whooshing sound as it begins sucking up the air.

I only mention this because that was the exact same noise that followed me taking off my dressing gown: the sound of

70 Greeted with the type of sympathetic applause usually reserved for horses that fall and break their necks in the Grand National.

two hundred people sucking in a great big gobful of air all at once. I turned and looked up at the balcony. Some of the mums were holding their hands over their mouths in horror. Others were covering the eyes of small children who were peering over the rail. A couple of the dads were stifling giggles. In the middle of it all, I located Mum. She was staring daggers at me.

What was going on?

The swimmers along the side of the pool were screaming with laughter. The announcer was babbling into the microphone: "Urgent towel needed on poolside. Repeat: urgent towel needed on poolside."

The mayor of the French town's face was a deep shade of purple and he looked like he was going to have a heart attack. He spat on the floor and yelled, "Pig. Disgusting English pig-dog. Why you insult France, you *merde*."

I repeat, what was going on?

"OW!"

A powerful hand grabbed me off the block by the shoulder and shoved me along the poolside. I guessed straight away that it was Dave King.

"You're sick, Martha, sick. Get out of here and NEVER COME BACK!"[71]

Embarrassed, confused and terrified, I ran along the slippery

---

71 This was not the first time that Dave had got my name wrong but it was definitely the first time that he had mistaken me for a girl.

tiles, almost slipping over as I skidded round the corner into the changing rooms. The room echoed with the booing of the parents and the wild laughter and hooting of the swimmers. The photographer from the local paper snapped away at me as I passed him.

When I got into the changing rooms, I looked in the mirror. What was wrong with me? What was so offensive that everyone could react like that? There was nothing. Absolutely nothing. And then I noticed it: a tiny black mark on my shoulder. It seemed to be part of something bigger. This was strange. Heart thumping, I slowly turned my body around, twisting my neck so that I could see my back.

Ste's Revenge

OK. How can I explain this? On my back was a picture. A picture that stretched from the waistline of my shorts right up to my neck. A picture that was drawn in permanent marker. A picture of extreme detail that I knew had been drawn by my brother when I was asleep the night before.

A picture of, well, a man's *you-know-what*.

I began to breathe heavily. I had exposed an obscene tattoo to two hundred parents, every single member of two swimming clubs and the mayor of a small French town.

This was not just not good. This was very, very bad.

Mum Gets Mad

As soon as I set foot into the foyer of the leisure centre after getting dressed, Mum collared me.

"Oh, this is just perfect," she sneered. "Once again you humiliate our family."

"What do you mean, me?" I said, keeping my voice down as a group of swimmers tried to listen in. "Why would I draw one of those *things* on myself?"

Mum shook her head. "I have no idea. I am beginning to think that you might need some therapy."

I grabbed her hand. "Mum. It was *on my back*. How could I possibly have drawn it? I am not made of rubber."

Mum pursed her lips. "Well, you probably got that friend of yours, Paul Beary, to help you. He seems as obsessed by naked bodies as you are."

"What are you talking about? It was clearly Ste. The golden boy. He did it to get back at me for telling Lucy that he was cheating on her."

"Nonsense," she said, tossing her head back, "Ste would never do anything like that. He is a nice boy. It's a pretty low trick to bring him into this. Once again, you've shown your jealousy, upset that poor girl and brought shame on us with your smutty obsessions. Do you know, I even heard the French mayor talk about severing all ties with Preston after this? You have sparked an international crisis. Now get in the car before you find any other countries to offend."

Bad Publicity

On the Monday afternoon, the *Evening News* dedicated its front page to me, with the headline, "French Stick – Crazed Swimmer Taunts French Mayor With Lewd Body Art". In the attached photo, I was standing on the block with the French mayor screaming at me in the background.

The article went on to describe me as "from a family of exhibitionists, including one of the notorious nudists who caused a stir in the Flag Market last week". They did not have any quotes from me because, when the reporters came to the house on Saturday night, Ste told them I had been sent to Tajikistan in disgrace and would be working as a goat herd until I had learned my lesson or frozen to death in my yurt.[72]

The headmaster of the school had already rung the house on Sunday and told Mum that it would be best if I did not come in that week. Apparently, the French swimming club would be spending a few days in school as part of their cultural exchange trip and, after fielding an angry phone call from the mayor on Saturday evening, he did not think he would be able to guarantee my safety. Also, he did not want the local community to think that the school condoned crude tattoos.

---

72 This would have been much better than the truth, which was that I spent the rest of the weekend in my room, face buried in my pillow, avoiding contact with anyone. Despite using up an entire bottle of Mum's body cleanser and scrubbing my body with a loofah so vigorously that I actually drew blood, I could not get rid of the picture.

So, in short, I was suspended from school and was now a notorious figure in Preston. People were having debates about me on the local radio station.[73] Preston's mayor issued a grovelling apology to his French counterpart, whose spokesman said, "Monsieur Barthez has a weak heart. This shock could have been catastrophic for him."

At about four o'clock on the Monday, Paul Beary came round and told me all about his day at school.

"You'll never guess what," he said, tipping the Smarties that he had brought for me down his own throat. "When those French swimmers came round school today, I got chatting to one of the girls."

"Oh really," I said.

Paul licked his lips. "Yeah, she was well gorgeous too."

"What a surprise," I yawned.

He did not seem to notice the sarcasm. "Yeah, she was just like that French girlfriend I used to have. I think she fancies me as well. Anyway, turns out that we're both going to the same party at the mayor of Preston's house tomorrow before the torchlit parade."

The torchlit parade. I had not even thought about it all weekend. It was in two days. I had been looking forward to

---

73 Most said I was a disgrace to the town. One even declared that, if I ever returned from Tajikistan, I should be strung up "like a pig in a butcher's window". However, one woman said that I was spot on and it was about time someone flashed a picture of a willy at some French people. I think she was drunk.

protecting Lucy. Now I knew there was no way I would be taking part. Something inside me snapped.

"Rubbish," I said.

"What?" said Paul, his face screwed up like a giant toddler's.

"What you just said. It was a load of rubbish. Why do you lie all the time? This French girl did not fancy you. She probably did not even exist. You are not going to the mayor's house either. You are full of—"

"Shut up!" cried Paul, looking hurt. "You don't know anything. I *am* going to the mayor's house. It's a buffet to celebrate the Preston Guild. All of the important people in Preston are going. I'm going with my uncle because he invented—"

"The caravan? NO. HE. DID. NOT. Your granddad was not the first person to be called Nathan. You have never found a finger with a life of its own in a sausage roll. No French girl has ever been out with you and never will. Your mum was not nearly abducted by aliens and you have never seen a ninja. You lie about everything and you get me into trouble all the time! If you had not opened your big gob about Ste and Lucy, he would not have drawn that . . . monstrosity on my back and I would not now be an international hate figure. Do you know what it is like to be stuck in here, frightened to go outside for fear a French sniper might be waiting for me?"

Paul scrunched up his face even more. "You're an idiot. No sniper would care about you. And I should know. My cousin *is* one."

"Liar."

"True, actually. I never lied once. For your information, that girl is real, she does fancy me and I'll prove it. Tomorrow night at the torchlit parade. You'll see."

"What will I see?" I said, but he had already stormed out of my room to the front door.

Great. Now I had upset my one and only friend. Things were definitely at rock bottom.

Things Drop Below Rock Bottom

As soon as Paul left, I felt so low that I decided to make myself an early tea and eat it on my bed. It was spaghetti hoops on toast and I could only face a couple of mouthfuls. Not wanting any more, I decided to sneak the plate downstairs to tip the rest into the bin. Just as I was about to step out of my room, I heard voices from downstairs in the hallway.

I poked my head round my door frame. Underneath the disgusting portrait of Mum and Dad, Ste was talking to Lucy. She was still looking tired and the bruise on her eye was starting to turn yellow.

What was she doing here? I had been worrying about her

all weekend. My only comfort was that she might never speak to Ste again. I hoped she was here to tell him what a dirty dog he was.

". . .and I've been crying non-stop all weekend. Dad's been on at me for losing the race; he wanted to know if it was you I was upset about and if it was you were dead. I've had to lie to him and say I was just upset because I was stressed out with training and wanting to win, otherwise. . ." she said, her voice cracking.

"Baby," said Ste, "I told you. That film was like six months old. That was a girl I knew ages ago. I've forgotten about her. I promise. She's nothing. You are the only girl for me."

"Well, why did Mike and his friend show me it then?"

Ste lowered his voice. "Look. Mike is mental. I know you think he's sweet but he is seriously messed up. Look at what he did to that mayor."

The *miscreant.*

Lucy laughed a little bit through her tears. "I read about that. Well, I suppose that *was* a bit strange. But how can I trust you?"

Ste grabbed both sides of her face. "Look at me. The Stevenator is a one-woman guy. He does not mess around with other girls. Don't worry about it. You wanna know where I was all those times when I said I was playing football and all that?"

"Yes, I do," she said, softly.

"I was making this. For you."

What Ste did next took me totally by surprise. He reached down and handed Lucy a bag that was tucked behind the curtain by the front door.

Lucy looked at him strangely and rustled around inside. She pulled out a carved wooden box. "It's. . ."

". . .stupid. I'm sorry," said Ste. "You can throw it away if you want."

"No," said Lucy, "It's beautiful. Why. . .? I mean, how. . .?"

Ste smiled. "Look. Don't tell anyone, but I enrolled on a woodwork course so I could make you something. Sad, I know, but *hey* – I'm just a guy in love. It's for all your medals. See how I carved your name in the top with a dolphin under it."

A knot grew in my stomach. This could not be true. Surely it had not happened. I did not want to believe it at all. Every molecule in my body said that it was not possible, but the evidence was right there in Lucy's hands: Ste had done something *nice*.

This was even worse than him doing something horrible. He had covered up for what a terrible human being he is by doing something *sweet*, maybe even *romantic*. Typical. What a greasy slimeball!

Why could I not have thought of it first?

Lucy looked like she was about to cry. "Oh my God. How long did this take you?"

"Oh, not long. About forty hours or so of solid work."

The knot in my stomach tightened. Maybe I *was* wrong about him. Maybe Paul's video *was* old. Of course: Paul wanted to be my friend again. He would do anything to try and make me forgive him. Like showing me what a terrible person Ste is.

This was an absolute disaster. Now Ste had somehow proved to Lucy that he was nice, she would *never* dump him. They would probably get married and I would have to carry the rings into the church on a little velvet cushion and every year for the rest of my life I would have to sit opposite them at Christmas dinner whilst they giggled and held hands under the table and fed each other roast potatoes from their forks. And then one day they would have children and Ste would train them to bite me.

Awful. Simply awful.

Lucy threw her arms round him. Ste caught my eye as he looked over her shoulder. He stuck his middle finger up at me whilst patting her on the backside with his other hand.

The baboon. He was still horrible underneath, box or no box. If only she could find out.

"Are you training tonight, babe?" he said, kissing her on the cheek. One eye was still pointing at me.

"No, Mum made Dad give me the week off. He's not totally happy but she made him accept that it might help me at the Nationals."

"Cool. Wanna go for a spin in the Love Mobile?"

Lucy playfully punched Ste in the arm. "I told myself I wouldn't, but. . ." Her face broke into a smile. "How can I turn down a man who made me such a beautiful box?"

He kissed her on the lips.

I fell back into my room and reached for my inhaler. If a meteorite had hit the Earth and destroyed mankind at that moment, I genuinely do not think it would have made things worse than they already were.

Chatting With Chas

Session 11 Transcript

Location and people present as Session 3

Chas: So, Mikey, we're going to get you to relax and take you back to find out where all of this started. I think that it might help you because, from there, we can confront your problems. How're you feeling?

[Eight-second pause. Chas lights a candle.]

POM: Michael. Have some squash. You look very pale.

MS: [*Has a drink.*] OK. I am ready. Please can we get it over with?

Chas: Right then, Michael. I want you to focus on this candle flame. Ignore everything else apart from the flame and my voice. And as I speak you find that your eyelids are becoming heavier and heavier and your body is relaxing more and more. And as this happens your arms and legs become lighter. And as they become lighter you feel yourself drifting, drifting slowly into a state of deep relaxation. Now I am going to ask you to raise your right arm.

MS: [*Raises right arm.*][74]

Chas: Excellent. Now, Michael, imagine all of your memories as being tucked away somewhere inside your mind. Imagine yourself flicking through them like an old photo album. Your first time on a bicycle. Your most recent birthday. Your first day at high school. I want you to reach back through all of those memories and find one in particular.

MS: Which one?

Chas: There is one memory that you may have locked away somewhere where you would not normally see it. It is from when you were very young and you took a donkey ride on a beach. Can you find that memory for me, Michael?

---

74 I do not remember this happening at all.

[Five-second pause.]

MS: Yes.

Chas: OK. Now I want you to imagine for me that you're right there, and tell me all about what is happening.

MS: I am on the beach. We are on holiday. Mum puts me on a donkey. I like it. The donkey does a poo.

Chas: [*Laughs.*] Very good, Michael. You like the donkey?

MS: Yes. The donkey is nice. But Ste is behind the donkey. I wave to him but he does not wave back. He smiles. Then he slaps the donkey on the bottom. It starts to run. The man and Mum try to stop it but it is too quick. I do not like it. It is out of control. Sand is spraying up everywhere. It is all going in my eyes. Mum and the man are screaming. I am trying to hold on but it is hard. Oh no! There is a fence up ahead. The donkey stops. I am flying through the air. I land right on the other side. My chin hurts but I do not cry. Oh no!

Chas: What is it, Michael?

MS: Everywhere there are people. They are all staring at me. I do not like this. It is horrible. Out of control. Pain in my chin. Blood on my T-shirt. Crazy donkey. And now the people. . .

Chas: What about the people?

MS: They are not wearing clothes. They are all in

the nudeys. They are all staring at me. I do not like it. Men, women, children, babies. They have got their own little bit of beach. They crowd around me. They are too close. I want to get away but I cannot. There are naughty bits everywhere and I have got a sore chin and I do not like it. There is a girl a bit bigger than me. She gives me a custard cream. I am scared to take it but she smiles. She looks nice. She makes me feel better. I am about to eat it but a man picks me up and I drop it in the sand. I look in his face and. . . Ah ah ah. I cannot breathe. I do not like the man. I do not like the man.

Chas: OK, Michael, calm down, calm down. I am going to count to three. With each number you will move further and further and further from the beach and back into this room. One . . . two . . . three, and relax. Miss O'Malley, another glass of squash for Michael.

[End of transcript]

After Hypnosis

That was seriously unsettling! I have just got home and I am still trembling. It was all so real. Chas said I had done very well and that he had known all along that the donkey thing was important. I had never remembered the bit about the nudists before. Chas said that I had probably blocked it out. People sometimes do that with traumatic experiences. He thought that this event may have made me:

1) Obsessed with order and being in control.
2) Scared of hooved animals.
3) Totally against nudity.
4) Frightened of being looked at.

He thought that the pain in my chin probably made all of those things stick in my memory even more. Because I was in pain, I ended up making a bigger issue of everything. "For your whole life," he said, nodding importantly, "you have associated all of those things with pain."

Anyway, he said that we had our answers now and that we would only have one more session. Then it would be down to me to confront my problems and sort them out myself.

Miss O'Malley told him he was a genius and that she would like to treat him to a cup of tea and a scone for all he had done for me. At that moment, I decided to leave. I guess that maybe Miss O'Malley had confronted some of her issues as well.

I am now sitting at home with the laptop and a packet of custard creams, waiting for Mum to get home from the shops. I decided to bring it home today. I want to finish writing my story before she arrives. Then I am going to talk to her properly for the first time in weeks and she is going to tell me everything.

I did not like what I saw when I was looking into the face of that man on the beach and I want an explanation.

The Mystery Plot

OK. So here is the last part of my story: the final events in the worst few weeks of my life.

When I left off last time, Ste had just kissed Lucy and made a rude gesture at me. I was slumped in my room, trying to avoid an asthma attack. As I heard Ste and Lucy driving away, I was at an all-time low. The Best Girl in the World had just taken my brother back after he cheated on her. My mum was a notorious nudist. I was suspended from school for being an international outcast.

I decided to move out.

When I say out, I mean *outside*. We have a tent in the garage that we used to use for camping holidays when we were younger. I could not take any more of the nudity and the being told off and the sliminess of my brother. I had about an hour and a half of daylight left – just enough time to pitch up in the back garden and get away from all of them.

I went downstairs to ask Mum whereabouts in the garage

the tent was. Through the back window, I could see that she was in the garden, talking on her mobile. Knowing that I was finally going to do something about this whole mess, I almost did not care that she was completely nude.[75]

"Mum," I said, as I walked outside, my eyes pointing no lower than her face.

"Not now, Michael," she said, waving me away irritably before going back to her call.

I decided to wait where I was, checking out the garden for where would be the best place to pitch my new home.

"Oh please, we need you," said Mum down the phone. "Without your planning, Operation Fig Leaf would have been a disaster."

My ears pricked up. She was talking to Dave King. Maybe I could shout something about Ste cheating on Lucy; then he would stop them from seeing each other.

". . .No, it's *not* a step too far. This is just a chance for us to open up to a wider audience. We must attack people's senses."

A step too far? Attack people's senses? What was she on about? I was now shamelessly listening in on her conversation.

"But Dave, how else can we show people that the law is wrong? Why can't we do what we like? . . . It is not wrong. . . No, I don't care about your other commitments. . . This is our

75 The key word here is "almost". I will not lie – the sight of her not wearing anything made me feel sick. It is just that, in my determination, I was prepared to swallow it down and get on with things.

best chance yet. . . Don't tell me what I can't do. . . OK, first my husband, then that art teacher and now you. . . Well, I'll just have to go it alone."

She angrily jabbed her finger down to end the call, then started pacing up and down the lawn muttering to herself, her eyes wildly flicking from side to side. She looked like a complete lunatic.

I raised my hand to get her attention. "Mum, what are you. . .?"

"Quiet, Michael. I'm thinking."

I went inside and found Dad sitting on the sofa, chewing his fingernails.

"What on Earth has got into Mum now?" I said.

Dad shook his head. "Don't ask, son. Don't ask."

The Tent

After rooting through the garage for ages, I finally found the tent. It was very difficult to set it up on my own because:

A) The poles kept popping out of place and falling down.

B) There was nobody to hold it down so every tiny gust of wind would carry the flysheet across the garden.

C) At least half of the pegs were missing.

D) I could not read the instructions because Ste had

scrawled across them in permanent marker: "IOU 7 pegs – needed 4 footy nets. Soz." The date he had written underneath was four years ago. Of course he had never bothered to put them back.

It was starting to get dark and I had still not made any progress when something very interesting happened. Dad, who I guess must have been watching through the window, came outside with a mallet. Without saying a word (or even looking at me at all) he expertly pitched the tent, using old bricks in place of the missing pegs to weigh down the guy ropes.

Once he had finished, he took a deep breath and said, "I hope that there'll be less bother for you out here than in the house."

With a sad, friendly nod, he patted me on the shoulder and ambled back inside.

I knew he was on my side.

No Longer Friends

Pleased with my new living arrangements, I decided to put on a disguise and ride my bike to the shops.[76] If I was going

---

76 This comprised Ste's sunglasses and a leather jacket from Dad's wardrobe that smelled about forty years old. The disguise actually looked even more rubbish than it sounds but I hoped it might put off any angry French people who may have been lying in wait for me.

camping in the back garden then I was going to need some custard creams. Mum was so distracted with her own thoughts that she forgot I was grounded. As I pushed my bike out of the garage, Ste pulled up in his car. Lucy was in it.

"Oh dear," I said.

As soon as she saw me, she leapt out of the passenger door. "Who do you think you are?" she snapped, her bruised eye now an angry yellow colour.

"I do not know," I said, backing myself up against the garage.

"Why did you and your stupid mate show me that video? I lost a race because of you and I almost lost my boyfriend. I thought you were my friend."

The last bit hurt the most.

"But I did not mean to upset you," I said, realizing that I sounded all whiny.

Lucy poked me in the chest with her finger. "What? You thought I'd be happy? Your friend has a film of Ste kissing a girl from, like, two million years ago and you think I'm going to want to watch it. What is your problem?"

If I had possessed even a shred of self-respect, I would have told her:

A) As far as I knew, the video was taken last week.
B) No matter how many boxes he carved, Ste would still never be good enough for her.

C) I only ever showed it to her because I want what is best for her.

D) Her friendship is one of the most important things in my life and I would never, ever do anything to hurt her.

Instead I kind of mewed like a runty kitten.

"You know what," she said, "I forgave you for spying on me with your friend. I even forgave you for the black eye. I felt sorry for you and I thought you were sweet. Well, you're not. You're a freak."

Ste nodded. "Come on, Luce. Let's get away from him."

With that, they both walked towards the front door.

"No!" I cried. "Mum is in there. She is not wearing anything."

Lucy stopped dead and spun around. "As if I care. Grow up."

I felt like I had been kicked in the spleen.

Sleeping Rough

Feeling numb, I cycled to the shops as slowly as I could. When I got home, Ste and Lucy were upstairs. Mum was in the front room, literally bouncing with excitement.[77] Dad tried to talk to

---

77 And I *mean* bouncing. I had to leave the room.

her but she just waved him away. At that point I took my cue to get my things together and go outside to the garden. That night I stayed in the tent for the first time, huddled under my duvet with a freezing cold nose.

Mum did not seem to notice.

She did not bother to come and see me once. In fact, every time I peered out of the tent flaps and saw her through the back window of the house, she was wearing this gormless grin, as though she was enjoying a joke that nobody else knew about. This made me very suspicious.

I had the worst night's sleep of my life. The same three thoughts kept buzzing around my head like angry wasps:

A) How could I possibly get Lucy away from Ste?
B) How could I get Lucy to be my special friend again and offer me hugs *and* kisses like she used to?
C) What on Earth was Mum up to?

A) and B) seemed like total lost causes. I had blown my chance of getting her to leave him and there was no way that she was ever going to talk to me again. With one hand-carved box and a couple of lies, Ste had secured her for life. As for C), well, whatever it was, it was obviously much worse than the naked art thing in the Flag Market and quite frankly that had been the worst moment of my life (so far). The three things ate away at me all night and, when I finally shoved my head out of the tent in the morning, I was so down that I even ate a custard cream for breakfast.

A Glimmer of Hope

Since I was still suspended, I did not have to go to school that day. I stumbled back into the house in my pyjamas with heavy eyes and my duvet wrapped around my shoulders. By the looks and sounds of things, Ste was in the shower, Dad had already gone to work, and Mum? Well, I had no idea where she was – I was just glad she was not nude and not at home.

I opened the kitchen bin to throw away my empty custard creams packet.[78] Something poking out from underneath the carrot peelings caught my eye. It was a flattened cardboard box with a picture of dolphins on it.

Something about the dolphins looked familiar. I fished it out, taking care not to brush against anything.

I could not believe it. It was a box. For a box.

What I mean is that this was a cardboard box that another box had been packaged in when bought from a shop.

When bought from a shop, I tell you.

The cardboard box said "Personalized Ocean Dream

---

78 OK, so I ate them all. I was depressed!

Jewellery Box. A gift for the special LUCY in your life" on it in big letters. The name "Lucy" was written in felt tip. On the packaging there was a big picture of a wooden jewellery box with cartoon dolphins leaping out of it. Underneath the picture were printed the four sweetest words in the English language.

"Hand-crafted in Bangladesh."

There could be no doubt about it whatsoever. This was the exact same wooden jewellery box that Ste had supposedly carved for Lucy at his woodwork class. How could Lucy and Iboth have been so gullible? Of course he had not made the box at all. He had not even been to a woodwork class. All he had done was buy her some crummy piece of junk and lied to her.

This was brilliant!

OK, it was a long shot but, if I could just get it to Lucy somehow, she would realize that he was a liar. Maybe she would ask him where he had really been all those times. Maybe then his house of cards would come tumbling down and she would forgive me and we would go back to sharing jokes about goggle marks and butterfly leg kicks.

She was obviously never going to talk to me, but if I could just get to her when she could not run away. . .

Of course! It was the torchlit procession that night. I could follow her float and give it to her at the end. And no one could say I was stalking her because I had already half-arranged to meet Paul Beary there.

Perfect.

The Glimmer Fizzles Out

"Rooting through the bins now you're homeless?"

Ste!

I quickly shoved the box under my duvet.

Ste sniffed. "Enjoying living outside? You know, now that you're out of the house, I might take Lucy into your room tonight after the torchlit procession. We could flick through the scrapbooks you've made of her. Then I could give her a good old-fashioned snog on your favourite rug."

I pretended not to care. "So you're going to be there, are you?"

I hoped he would. He had not seen the cardboard box in my hands at all. Imagine his face when I showed it to her.

Ste sniffed. "Not my thing. Anyway, Lucy's busy all evening on her float. I'll have the chance to get busy myself, if you know what I mean."

I felt like an icy finger had scratched my back. "You mean. . ."

Ste sneered at me. "Mike. There are billions of women in the world and only one of me. What else am I supposed to do when Lucy's swimming or trundling round on some stupid float? Every woman on Earth deserves a little piece of the Stevenator."

I was horrified. "I knew it. I knew it all along. You *are* cheating on her."

Ste looked at me like I was mental. "Course I am. The Stevenator does not get tied down. What are you going to do? Tell her? She'll never believe you. You're a freak, Mike. *A freak*. Not my words. The words of Lucy King."

"But you will make her sad again. She has the National Championships coming up. You could ruin her career."

He smoothed down a blob of ladies' make-up that was covering up a spot on his chin. "Which is exactly why she'll never find out. I'll drop off my other piece of fluff. Then I'll be in town to pick Lucy up after the procession and she'll be happy to see me and she won't know anything about what I've been doing. The end. Oh. And I'll have that cardboard box, thanks." He reached under the duvet and whipped it out of my hand. "We wouldn't want her to be *sad* again, would we? Not with the National Championships coming up."

He lightly slapped me on the cheek, gave me a wink and sauntered out.

The Torchlit Procession

I spent the rest of the day on my own, cooped up in the house, feeling depressed and comfort-eating another packet of custard creams. At about four-thirty, Mum rang and said that she would not be coming home at all until late that evening and could I get my own tea. Dad was not home from work and Ste was off canoodling somewhere.

A little later I got a text off Paul Beary asking me if I still wanted to meet up in town to watch the procession and be introduced to his French girlfriend. At first I did not want to go. The last person I wanted to see was Lucy going past, blissfully unaware of what Ste was doing behind her back. However, I said yes for three reasons:

1. I was seriously bored and fed up.
2. I was actually quite curious as to what lie Paul would create to cover up for the fact that his girlfriend did not exist.
3. If I stayed at home I would probably not have done much, apart from eating a third packet of custard creams.

On top of these reasons, it felt good to be ignoring Mum's orders that I should be grounded. Therefore, at about six-thirty, I was waiting on my own for the floats to come past. Predictably, Paul was late. Probably busy making up his ridiculous story, I guessed.

If you have never been to a torchlit procession, they are a bit like any other procession (i.e., boring), except they happen in the evening and each float (really just an old lorry with rubbish decorations on it) is led by a couple of people carrying flaming torches. These people pretend to pull the lorry with a piece of rope in their other hand but really everyone can tell that the engine is on and the person in the cab is clearly driving. This strikes me as completely pointless (as does the fact that they use torches in the first place, even though Preston has perfectly adequate street lighting).

I was by the side of the road, just outside the town centre. As I mentioned before, this torchlit procession only takes place once every twenty years. As a result it seemed like the whole town was outside to watch it. The pavements were teeming with people: adults straining their necks to watch, children sitting on their parents' shoulders or pressed up against the barriers by the side of the road.

I did not get what all of the people were doing there. I mean, I had a decent excuse – I was going to meet my obese friend to prove to myself that his French girlfriend did not exist and perhaps admire a talented athlete who hated me. They were just there to look at lorries made out to look like a jungle or a martial arts dojo or something silly like that. It made no sense.

Policemen in yellow jackets strolled up and down, some of them even eating candyfloss. Thinking ahead, I had sat on top of a four-foot-high wall that separated the pavement from a car park on the other side. I was just high enough to see over everyone's heads without being jostled about.

As predicted, the procession was DULL and the floats were RUBBISH. There was a brass band that went past sitting on their float, playing some depressing piece of music.[79] One of the primary schools had a float with a Christmas theme.[80] The Market Traders' Association was pretending to act out a medieval market scene.[81]

And so it went on. And on. And on. Float after boring float, each one greeted by inexplicable wild cheering from the crowd. Still, there was no sign of the swimming club float. I was seriously considering giving the whole thing up when I got a tap on my leg.

"Hey, Mike."

I looked down. It was Paul Beary. He was holding the hand of a girl. A real, live, human girl. She was even good-looking. My mouth dropped open.

"Mike," he grinned, "this is Chantelle. She's one of the. . ."

"French swimmers," I said, recognizing her from the gala. "Where did you. . ."

Paul ran a chubby hand through his hair. "I told you. At

---

79 The only highlight being when the trombonist's wig fell off in a gust of wind.

80 I will just mention that it was late September.

81 This really was the worst float of all. One of the medieval traders was wearing a baseball cap and talking on a mobile phone. The only reason I knew that it was a *medieval* market scene was the big sign along the side of the float that read: "Medieval Market Scene".

school. We met up at the mayor's house. I was there with my uncle and all of the other important people in the city."

I could not believe it. Maybe his uncle *had* invented the caravan after all. I mean, it *is* hard to believe when you consider all the other nonsense he spouts, but still. . .

The girl looked at him like he was a male model or something. "Paul is lovely. He tell me all about 'ow 'e once saved the mayor's life when someone tried to, 'ow you say. . ."

"Assassinate him," said Paul, winking at me.

"Oh yes," I said, flatly. "He does things like that all of the time."

"'Ang on," she said, her eyes widening, "You are the boy with the picture on 'is back of the—"

"Yes," I said.[82] "But listen. That was not me. Honestly. Please, tell everyone in France."

"Paul," she said, turning her nose up, "take me away from zis . . . dirty boy."

"Yes, of course," said Paul, wearily. "He's not really a friend of mine. I only know him through my charity work. I try to help people with sick minds get on in the world. And he is the worst case I have ever come across. Still. All I can do is try to make the world a better place."

Chantelle pursed her lips at me, then smiled at him. "Oh,

---

82 Despite two days of scrubbing, it was still there.

Paul. You are so sweet. It must be so 'ard to 'elp such . . . er . . . 'ow you say. . ."

Paul gave a wise nod. "I believe the word is 'freak'."

Freak again. Unbelievable. First Lucy and now him as well.

He led her off into the crowd, nodding at me over his shoulder and mouthing the word "PHWOARR". I had seen the expression on his face many times before – a kind of mix between uncontrollable hunger and rabid excitement. It also occurs when he is sitting directly in front of a huge slice of chocolate cake.

As he disappeared, I rubbed my eyes and took a deep puff on my inhaler. Was everyone else on Earth just here to ruin my life?

A big cheer from the crowd greeted another float. I looked up. It was the Preston Piranhas Swimming Club.

The Swimming Club's Float

As already mentioned, the swimming club float had an "under the sea" theme. This included:

1. Blue shiny paper on the back of the lorry.
2. A stereo playing "Under the Sea" from *The Little Mermaid*. This kept skipping every time the lorry went over a bump and so did not actually get past the chorus.

3. People dressed as fish, mermaids and other undersea creatures. There were no sea slugs.
4. Lucy as the queen of the sea, the bruise on her eye still slightly visible. She was sitting on a throne, wearing a crown, a bikini top and a fish's tail. She looked lovely, even though I was more interested in how majestic she looked as a member of the aquatic royal family. I mean, I knew she was a great swimmer but I had no idea that she could act as well.
5. Dave King driving the lorry dressed as Popeye.

The float crawled past at a snail's pace, everyone whooping and cheering. Forgetting myself, I waved at Lucy. She seemed to notice me but she was too focused on staying in character to wave back.

An Unforeseen Problem

Just as the float was drawing level with me, there was a kerfuffle on the far pavement. A woman had burst through the barrier. She leapt on to the back of the float and opened up a big flag that read: "Proud to be Free".

She was wearing a mask. Apart from that, she was completely naked.

I almost fell off the wall. "Mum!"

Time to Do Something

Half the crowd were laughing; the other half were booing her. She carried on waving her flag. Terrified, most of the swimmers managed to scramble off the side of the float. Lucy could not move, though. She was stuck because of her fish tail.

"Dad! Stop the float!" she wailed. He did not seem to hear her.

Without a sea slug on board, there was nobody to protect her. I had to do something. This should have been *my* job, after all.

I pushed my way through the crowd and struggled over the barrier, then ran up alongside the lorry. I swung my foot up on to the side, hauled myself up and yanked open the door.

"Myron!" growled Dave, staring at me incredulously. "What the hell are you doing?"

I bundled myself into the cab. "My name is Michael," I said, firmly. "Stop the float. You must stop the float. There is a maniac on board."

"Yeah. You," snarled Dave. "Now sod off."

At that moment I did something very stupid. Something that I would never recommend to anyone.

I flung myself across the cab and shoved my hand down on the brake pedal. Unfortunately, I made two fundamental errors:

1. It transpires that, by mistake, I actually shoved my hand down on the accelerator pedal. This caused the lorry to lurch forward.
2. I tripped on the gearstick and somehow managed to get my big wobbly head jammed between Dave's knees and the steering wheel. I tried desperately to wriggle free. Dave tried desperately to haul me free by my hair.

In the struggle, the leather steering wheel slowly turned to the right, dragging across my cheek. The lorry followed. Dave swore and grabbed the wheel but it was locked in place by my head. I could not move. His foot went for the brake but my body was pinning his leg down and he could not move it. My hand was still pressed against the accelerator. We were heading off the road. He pounded the horn. People on the pavement screamed. There was a bump as the float mounted the kerb, the sound of the mangled metal barrier being dragged under the wheels, the deep thud of a brick wall being crushed, a shuddering jolt as the lorry dropped down a foot or so. With a loud roar, Dave shoved my body out of the way with his leg, then stamped down.

The brakes squealed.

There was a long, drawn-out metallic crunch.

The float stopped dead, flinging me forward into the footwell.

"You idiot!" barked Dave, as I scrambled out of the way.

Lucy's face appeared in the window at the back of the cab. Her crown was all wonky on her head and her hair was all over the place. She put her hand over her mouth. "Oh my God. You hit a car."

I was glad of this distraction because it stopped Dave from throwing me out on to the street. Very slowly, we turned to look out of the front window.

As the dust settled, it gradually became clear that, yes, we had completely mangled the front end of a car. A black car, whose bonnet was so twisted that its personalized number plate was pointing up in the air so that we could clearly read it. A black VW Golf, to be precise, number plate "C00L S1E", with two screws either side of the 1 to make it look like a T.

Two people were sitting inside.

Neither of them seemed to be hurt, but the force of the crash had pinned them back in their seats, stuck in the position they had been sitting in beforehand. The young man in the driver's seat had his arms around the young lady next to him, and their lips were very close to each other.

"Ste," all three of us said at the same time.

"I'll kill him," Dave said, flinging the lorry door open.

In the car, Ste was desperately trying to get out and escape. Behind me, Lucy was wailing.

With one punch, Dave shattered the driver's window of the car, then dragged Ste out through it by his shoulders. I hid my eyes. There followed a series of dull thumps and loud moans.

When I dared to look back, about ten policemen were pulling Dave away. My brother was on his knees, blood dripping from his nose, his shirt torn across the front. The injuries did not seem to bother him as much as the wreck of his Golf, though.

"My car. My beautiful car," he cried.

Ste was completely distracted by the wreckage, and he did not notice Lucy walking over until she was right next to him. She had removed her fish tail and was now wearing just a bikini.

"Babe," he said, struggling to his feet, "this isn't what you think. I was giving her a lift. I was just about to come and watch you on your float. Honestly I was. She had something in her eye and I was trying to get it out."

Lucy drew her arm back and delivered a stunning right hook to Ste's nose. His eyes turned in on themselves. He wobbled round a few times before his knees buckled and he collapsed on to the ground with a crunch.

Lucy marched over to her dad, who, having seen her punch Ste's lights out, had finally calmed down.

"I told you he was no good," growled Dave. "No wonder you lost that race. Worrying about him all the time. Boys will cost you your career, you know that?"

Lucy's bottom lip wobbled. "Career? Is that all you care

about? You make me train day in, day out. You control me. You don't even ask me if I'm OK when someone treats me like a piece of dirt. Well, I don't want a stupid career in swimming. I don't want to train any more. I'm sick of it. I quit."

I had an overwhelming urge to go and help her. To give her that hug she had promised me. But before I could move, she had stormed off into the crowd. Dave made a break for her but the police officers pulled him back. I slid out of the cab as she disappeared into the sea of people.

Behind me, there was another scuffle. A second group of police officers were trying to restrain Mum.

"Let me go!" she cried. "I am a human being. This is what a human being looks like. You are arresting me for being in my natural state."

"No," said one of the female police officers, calmly, "we are arresting you for public indecency and causing a disturbance."

Mum suddenly became very agitated. "Look, please don't arrest me. I got the wrong float. I'm sorry. This was meant to be a peaceful protest. I wanted the float with the judges from the law courts on it. I didn't mean to get on this one. I wanted them to change the laws. I just want to be allowed to be naked. To be free to walk round as nature intended. I couldn't see which float I was getting on because of the mask. My husband is over there. He'll explain everything. Roy. Help me."

"Course he will," said the police officer, leading her firmly away.

I picked Dad out in the front of the crowd. "I tried to stop her but she wouldn't listen," he said, shaking his head sadly as the door of the police van closed behind her.

The End

So that is the end of the story. Mum spent a night at the police station and, when she came out, she and Dad had a Big Talk. Five days later, I had my first session with Miss O'Malley. Since then, thank heavens, Mum has not been naked in the house again. The horror of the whole nudist thing still burns in my brain, though.

Two days after the procession, Ste went to Australia to stay with our uncle until the whole thing blows over. Mum paid for the ticket as an advance on the insurance money from his car. He was planning to go after his A levels anyway but he has brought it forward. I do not know or particularly care when he is going to return.

To my knowledge, Dave and Lucy King have not been seen at the swimming club since.

I feel slightly better for finishing the story. But, as I am sitting here, the laptop battery red-hot from being on for so long and an empty custard cream packet folded neatly on the side of my desk, there is still one thing I must speak to Mum about. There is no way the story can be properly finished until she explains about the man on the beach once and for all.

(*Twenty Minutes Later*)
Mum Comes Home

The moment after I finished typing that last sentence, Mum came back from the shops. The click of the door closing was like a switch, flicking me back in time: the beach, the donkey, the man's face. I needed to find out.

Immediately, I took a puff on my inhaler, shut down the laptop and confronted her at the front door.

"Why did you never tell me?" I said. I could feel my face getting hot.

"Tell you what?" she sighed.

"About the day that I got thrown off the back of that donkey when I was five?"

Mum rolled her eyes. "What are you talking about now?"

"That's when it all started, isn't it? The moment I landed in that nude party is the moment you started all this, this, this, naked nonsense."

Mum's eyes widened. "How did you. . .?"

I shrugged.

She took a deep breath. "I didn't mean to upset you with

this. I didn't want you to get hurt."

"Well, you did upset me. And I did get hurt," I said. "And now I want you to explain."

There was a long pause. After a while, Mum took a deep breath and looked at the floor.

"I'm sorry," she said. "We were on holiday in Devon, on the beach. One minute, you were there on the donkey. The next moment, you were gone."

"Because Ste hit it on the bum."

Mum smiled sadly. "Maybe. Anyway, we chased it right across the beach until it came to this fence. Then it kind of stopped dead and threw you over. I was petrified. I ran over and there you were. . ."

"Surrounded by naked idiots," I said.

"Well, that's one way of looking at it. You were in a nudist part of the beach, separated from the rest of it. And you were being held by a man. Loads of people were around you, making a fuss. There was blood all over you and you were crying but I guessed you were all right. Someone had even given you a biscuit. And then, when I saw you were OK, I noticed everyone else. They looked so. . ."

"Disgusting?"

Mum did not seem to register what I had said. ". . .happy. I was shocked. I mean, I'd never seen anything like that before. And compared to me, completely frazzled from looking after two young boys, they were just so *free*, and I totally understood what they were doing."

"Getting sunburn on their bits?"

"No. Breaking free. Forgetting the rules. Getting out and doing what they wanted. I was so jealous." She allowed herself a little smile. "And I must have been standing there for ages because the man who was holding you suddenly said something like, "This yours?" in this really gruff voice and shoved you into my arms. And it was. . ."

I shuddered as I remembered the man's face from when I was hypnotized. "Dave King."

"Yes," she said quietly. "Well, I didn't know who he was then, of course. He was just a man with no clothes on."

"Huh."

Mum sighed. "Anyway. The holiday finished and we went home. I couldn't think of anything else for ages but how happy and free those people were. My life with all its rules and hard work just seemed so drab. Then, around a year or so later, when I was taking you for a splash around in the baby pool at the leisure centre, I saw him."

"Who?"

"Dave. He was coaching in the big pool, screaming at Lucy, who was only about seven or so at the time. He was wearing clothes but I recognized him straight away. I couldn't believe it was him. Right here in Preston. So, that day, I signed you up for the swimming club."

I took a deep puff on my inhaler. "You mean to say, I have been forced into swimming for the last eight years so that you could go round in the nude?"

Mum's eyes widened. "No. It wasn't like that. . . Well, OK, it kind of was like that. Soon you were swimming three times a week. I would always come to try and get close to Dave, to talk to him, find out about the nudism, but I could never bring myself to ask him about . . . *that*. I mean, what could I say? 'Hello. Remember me from the nudist beach? I was the one peering over the fence.' He might think I was stalking him. Once you've failed to bring that sort of thing up with someone the first few times, you've lost your chance. Oh, the hours I've spent on that balcony, thinking about what I could say to him about it."

"So you *did* fancy him, then."

Mum looked genuinely hurt. "No! Absolutely not. I am married to your father, Michael. But I was, well, *fascinated* by him. How did he have the courage to do *that*? All of that time, your father and I would take one morning a week to just try it at home. Always on a Saturday when we knew you would be out. It became a routine, I suppose."

"But Dad did not want to."

"No," she shrugged, "but he did it for me. We carried on like that for years. Anyway, after that day that you caught us here, I just felt like something had been lifted. It was all in the open. It reignited that desire for freedom in me. But this time

I was determined to seize the moment. I found out that Dave did an art class and that was it. I signed your father and me up as models straight away. After that, it just got out of control."

"But *why* did you follow Dave around like that?"

"Oh, Michael. I was trying to find out his secret. How had he managed to feel so free back then? The funny thing is, I've found out since that he gave up the whole naked thing almost straight after that holiday so that he could focus on Lucy's swimming. He's not even a nudist any more."

"Well, why did he help you, then?"

"Oh, I don't know. I think that organizing Operation Fig Leaf reminded him of being in the army. You know, that's probably why he gets so angry. Without people to scream at or shoot at, he feels anxious. Even so, he thought the whole thing was getting out of hand. And he thought it was wasting time he could have been training Lucy. Look, Michael. I'm so sorry about everything."

I shook my head, then walked back upstairs. I do not think I am ready to forgive her yet.

After

That conversation happened this afternoon. I am now in bed. The thing is, I do not feel any different. Chas told me that I needed to confront my problem. I thought I had, but I still feel bad about everything. I mean, I tested myself by looking at a picture of a donkey on the internet before. I thought I was going to have a heart attack. The mere thought of everything that happened with my parents gives me a serious case of the creeps and I am still worried about Lucy too. I have still barely seen her since the torchlit procession.

Tomorrow is my last session with Chas. I hope that he can sort this out.

Chatting With Chas

Session 12 Transcript

Location as Session 3
People present as Session 3, plus Lucy King (hereafter "LK")

Chas: Hello there, Michael.

[Five-second pause.]

Chas: Michael. I think you know Lucy.

MS: Yes.

LK: I thought you were seeing *me* at two. Have I made a mistake?

Chas: No mistake at all, Lucy. I have also been having sessions with Michael for the last few weeks.

LK: I suppose he could do with it.

MS: Also? You mean you've been meeting her all this time as well?

Chas: Of course.

POM: I asked him to.

Chas: Yes. The beautiful Miss O'Malley thought you could both do with a little help in getting back on track.

MS: You could have told me.

Chas: Never heard of confidentiality?

[Three-second pause.]

LK: So why do you want us both here now?

Chas: Well, I told both of you that this would be your final session.

MS: Yes.

Chas: And I told both of you that, in order to get to the bottom of the way you were feeling, we had to confront whatever it was that was making you feel like this.

MS: And. . .

Chas: Here we are. Michael, from what Lucy tells me, your brother was a major reason for her recent problems.

MS: Yes. He is an idiot.

LK: Exactly.

Chas: But, more than this, Lucy, being forced into swimming training your whole life has been a far bigger problem.

LK: Yes. It just got too much, you know. I wasn't doing it for myself. I wasn't having fun.

MS: Me too. I found out yesterday that the only reason I have been forced to swim all these years is so that my mum could get close to Lucy's dad, who used to be a nudist.

LK: [*Laughs.*] Oh my God. I'm glad he gave that up. Mum and I still laugh about it.

MS: I do not find it quite as funny.

[Five-second pause.]

Chas: OK. So you both have problems that are interlinked. After the last session had finished, and you had told me what you had seen during your trance, Michael, I realized that your problem started when you first met Lucy about nine years ago.

MS: I did not say that.

LK: What is he talking about?

Chas: But I thought it must be obvious. . .

[Fourteen-second pause.]

MS: Hold on. It *was* you! Of course. It *must* have been you.

LK: He's being strange again.

MS: You were the girl who gave me the custard cream.

LK: I really have no idea what you are on about.

MS: Neither did I until now. But it *was* you. Of course it was. It all makes sense.

LK: O-K. Does anyone want to tell me what this means? I'm starting to get a little uncomfortable. . .

Chas: Well, from the regression therapy session I had with Michael last week, it seems that the two of you first met by chance during a holiday with your respective families in Devon when you were six and Mikey was a little younger. It seems to me that these holidays were of particular significance in shaping both of your lives.

LK: Still don't follow.

Chas: Lucy, from what you have told me during our sessions, that holiday was very important for you. You said it was . . . [*Consults notes.*] . . . the last time you ever remember having swum for fun.

LK: Oh yes. It was in the sea. Mum's told the story about a million times. Dad had just left the army. He was drifting about, not knowing what to do, so he took us on a nudist holiday. I guess he thought that finally he didn't have to wear a uniform, so why should he wear anything? Anyway, we went to the beach and I just walked straight into the sea and started swimming in the waves. Apparently I was a natural. No rubber ring or armbands or anything. Dad was gobsmacked. Mum says that he said to her, "With the right coaching, she could be an Olympic gold medallist." And right then he knew what he wanted to do with the rest of his life. . .

MS: What?

LK: Train me up. Make me a champion. As soon as we got home he gave up the nudism, took every swimming-coaching course he could, got a job in Preston as head coach of the swimming club and the rest, well, I suppose you know about.

Chas: And Mike. The holiday started your mother's obsession with nudism and, through your painful donkey ride, sparked all kinds of fears in you. So. Like I have said before, we know what both of your problems are. We know where they have come from. It turns out that they both started at the same time. Now, you both need to go out there and confront them. How you do it is up to you, but I think you must do it together.

LK: No way.

Chas: Now, now. I think that this is your best chance. You can do it if you work together. As both of you are part of each other's problems, it will help you even more.

[Fifteen-second pause. LK shakes head, then shakes hands with MS. MS smiles. LK also smiles.]

Chas: OK, babes. We got a deal.

POM: [*Kisses Chas on the cheek.*] Wonderful, Chas. Absolutely wonderful.

MS: Wait. Are you two. . .?

[End of transcript]

That Night

After the session, Lucy and I went home separately. At about seven o'clock, my phone beeped. A text message. This was a massive surprise. The only texts I usually get are from Paul Beary (rude jokes), Ste (insults) or the swimming club (impersonal, automated messages when training is cancelled).

I checked my phone wearily, then immediately sat up straight. It was from Lucy. Lucy King. Where did she get my number? Of course I had hers.[83] My whole body shivered. It is

83 Source: scrap of paper found on my brother's desk after he left for Australia.

not every day that you get a message from a potentially world-class athlete.

"Hi Mike. How ru? Got a gr8 idea 2 sort probs. L x"

A *kiss.* Everyone knows that a kiss on a text is even better than a real one. Unlike a real kiss, which can be over in milliseconds (probably), a text kiss lasts for ever. Unless you delete the message, that is.

I am *never* going to delete this message. In ten million years, long after human beings have died out, aliens will colonize the planet. They will find my phone buried deep under the rubble of our collapsed civilisation, switch it on and see that the kiss from Lucy still exists.

My hands were shaking as I texted back: "Dear Lucy. It was a wonderful surprise to hear from you. What kind of an idea did you have in mind? Eternally yours. Michael."[84]

My fingers hovered over the number nine on my keypad for a moment. Should I do it? Should I? Should I really? With a surge of excitement, I prodded at it:

"X".

I pressed send before I had the chance to delete it.

Message Sent.

Suddenly I began to panic. I mean, it was a *capital letter* kiss. Is that not a bit aggressive? Would she think I was forcing a kiss on her, all uncontrollable lips and forceful tongue, like a

---

84 I do not use "text speak".

giraffe poking its head through a car window at a safari park? This was not good.

Covered in cold sweat, I started to compose a new message:

"Dear Lucy. Please forgive me for my over-exuberance. I did not wish to offend you, but. . ."

My phone beeped again.

Lucy!

Petrified, I cleared what I had been typing and opened the message.

"Ur funny. Lol ;).[85] B @ Preston train station on Sat @ 9 am. Bring swim shorts & towel. CU then love L x x x x"

Four kisses and a love!

I literally almost exploded.

I was so excited it took me almost five minutes to reply: "Dear Lucy. I will most certainly be there on Saturday at the suggested time. With love, Michael x x x x x"

Five kisses, Lucy. I hope your face is ready for them!

Postscript
Blackpool Beach

I am glad that it is foggy. It means that the beach is empty.

The donkey man does not want to let us borrow a donkey.

---

85 I believe that this counts as another wink, and one of the good kind at that.

He says we are too big. I tell him that Lucy weighs seven and a half stone and that she is light enough to ride it. She laughs and asks how I know. I say nothing.

I read it on the swimming club website.

He still looks dubious so I reach into my rucksack for my wallet and pay him double the price, from the money I cleared out of my account before getting on the train this morning. Lucy wants to pay half but I explain that this part of the morning is to solve my problems, not hers.

Lucy's idea was simple. She said that we should go to the beach and have fun. We should face our fears and our obstacles head-on. I did not wish to hire a donkey but she said it was important for me. When she said it, she squeezed my hand. I immediately agreed.

I am shaking as Lucy gets on the donkey. I feel sick but I swallow the tightness in my throat and begin to lead her along the beach with the rope.

As we walk along the water's edge, the donkey's bells and buckles jingling, I reach out a trembling hand and very lightly pat the donkey on its neck. A shudder of electricity shoots along my arms, from my fingertips all the way to my shoulder. Instantly I pull my hand away.

Nothing happens. I do not die. My hand does not turn green and fall off. The scar on my chin does not pulsate and erupt like a volcano.

I take a deep breath.

Very slowly, I place my hand back on to its fur, leaving it there this time. It feels warm and soft.

I smile and something comes over me. We are here to confront our problems but it is supposed to be fun. I cannot remember the last time I enjoyed myself.

"Come on!" I shout. I break into a run.

"You're crazy!" shouts Lucy, bouncing up and down as the donkey and I trot across the sand and into the calm, cold shallows by the pier.

"Here's perfect," she says.

"Perfect for what?" I say, slowing down then stopping.

Lucy does not answer me. She swings her leg over the side of the donkey and ties it to the wooden frame of the pier.

I look back towards the donkey man but I cannot see anywhere near far enough. The air is cold and salty.

"We've got to beat our problems sometime," she says. "I've got to learn to enjoy myself in the water. And you've got to. . ."

There is a funny smile on her face.

"I have got to what?" I say.

"Don't look," she says.

I turn around. There is the sound of clothes hitting the ground and then feet slap-slap-slapping against the wet sand.

When I turn back, she is sprinting into the sea, water splashing up all around her. As she dives into a wave, I cannot help but notice that she is wearing a bikini.

A bikini! That is not suitable swimming attire for a champion swimmer. It takes me a moment to remember that we are here to have fun, not to train.

"Oooh-ooh-ah-ah!" she laughs, after emerging from the dull grey water. "It's freezing."

She dunks her head under and kicks her legs up in the air before surfacing again. "Are you not coming in?"

I look around. In the fog, the donkey is the only thing that can see me. And he is lying down for a rest.

"OK," I say. "But no looking."

"I wouldn't dream of it," Lucy says, turning around, then ducking under the water.

"Here goes," I say. I am wearing my swimming shorts under my clothes. I slip my trousers off, take off my top and fold my clothes neatly inside my rucksack. I remove my shoes and put my watch inside one of them. I am in the water before I know it.

At first it is unbearably cold but we soon get used to it. We splash and dive and dip and kick and pull handstands and squirt water through our hands and laugh until our stomachs hurt.

After who-knows-how-much time, Lucy suddenly says: "Are you ready now, Mike?"

"Ready for what?"

She is still smiling. "Ready to face up to your problems?"

"That is what I am doing."

Lucy stops smiling. I suddenly notice how the waves cause my body to sway involuntarily.

"No, Mike," she says. "We're currently facing up to my problems. I am the one who needed to enjoy myself in the water. You needed to face up to your fear of donkeys. . ."

"Which I have done."

"Yes. And now, you have to face up to your other fear." She nods knowingly at me.

At first I have no idea what she means. Then, very slowly, I realize.

The water becomes freezing cold again. I look over to the donkey, which is calmly licking the heavy wooden frame of the pier. Something brushes against my foot and I flick it away. In the distance, I can hear a police siren. I am suddenly aware of how big the sea is.

"I cannot do that," I say, finally. "It is disgusting."

"No, Michael. You've got to."

"Why?" I say, crossing my arms over my chest. "I am happy. I am enjoying myself. I stroked a flipping donkey, for heaven's sake."

Lucy shakes her head slowly. "It isn't enough, Mike. You need to let go. If something scares you so much that it's ruined your life, then you need to face it head on. Otherwise, you'll be a slave to it for ever."

"How will doing . . . that help?"

"It'll make you realize that you are bigger than the problem. You are more powerful. You are in charge. The problem isn't in control here. You are."

"I do not agree with this. You sound like Chas."

Lucy grins. "Yeah. Like. Radical. Dude. Surf the wave of fear, Mikey."

"But I cannot," I say, not smiling even though her impression is very funny. "What if someone sees? What if you see?"

"I won't look," she says. "And anyway, A) there's nobody on the beach; B) it's foggy; and C) this water's so cloudy you can't see more than about two centimetres down."

"But. . ."

"Mike. You have to do it. No one will ever find out. I know you can do it. I believe in you."

She looks at me with her lovely brown eyes, salty water dripping down her eyelashes and on to her flushed cheeks.

"I do not want to."

"Just for ten seconds."

"And you promise you will not look."

"Michael. Why would I want to look?" she says, the beginnings of a smile creeping across her face.

Then she pecks me on the cheek.

A peck on the cheek. A real-life perfect peck from a real-life perfect girl. This is literally the best thing that has ever happened to anybody ever.

She theatrically puts her hands over her eyes and slowly turns around.

I take a deep breath, look around and check the water. She is right. I can hardly see the shore from here through the fog, and the water is so murky that nobody will see anything. My thumbs are shaking as I push them into the waistband of my shorts.

"No looking," I croak.

"Of course not," replies Lucy, ducking herself under the water. "But hurry up. I'm getting cold."

My whole arms are straining, as though trying to stop me from pushing downwards. There is a moment of tension. I cannot do this. I will not do this. But Lucy said I should do it. Lucy said it is the right thing to do. Lucy believes in me. Lucy. Lucy. Lucy.

With a triumphant cry, I pull my shorts down and hurl them over my head behind me.

I am nude.

"I've done it!" I scream. "I've done it. Don't turn around but I've done it!"

I do not know what I feel. Relief? Revulsion? Delight? Disgust? Happiness? Horror? All of them? None of them? It does not matter. Overall, I know I have won. I will never do this again but I have won. I am not scared any more. I am in charge. I am just a tiny little person in this great big sea but, for this one passing instantaneous moment, I am in charge.

"Well done, Michael," says Lucy, clapping her hands but still facing away.

"Don't look still," I say, "I'm going to get my shorts."

I turn around and swim back towards the shore.

ACKNOWLEDGEMENTS

Here are the people who have helped with the book. Without them I would never have finished it. And, if I had finished it, it would have been rubbish.

1) A big stack of custard creams to everyone at Scholastic. Thank you for taking a chance with an odd little book like this and an odd little man like me, and for all the hard work since. In particular, thanks to Alice, Clare and Andrew for being clever, patient and generally very nice, and to Jess for the giant biscuit.
2) Free donkey rides to my truly tremendous agent Gillie, without whom none of this would have been possible, and everyone else at Aitken Alexander.
3) Large portraits of nude people go to Steve Hawes for all the time, help and food when I was getting started, and Kathryn Ross for the superb feedback.
4) A dedicated torchlit parade to Mum, Dad, Rachel, James, David and all my nieces, nephews, uncles, aunties, cousins and in-laws for being brilliant, funny and nothing like the family in this book.
5) Invites to Operation Birdseye to Andy Melrose, Judy Waite, Lozano, Wilko and everyone else from the Winchester MA for teaching me to write real good.
6) A big naked jamboree in honour of my pals from Preston, Leeds, Cambridge and everywhere else, especially Swarbs and family. Thanks for the laughs.
7) Finally, nice lower-case kisses on the beach to Sarah and Jasmine for making me happy.

WWW.FACEBOOK.COM/THEREALMICHAELSWARBRICK

WWW.TWITTER.COM/REALMSWARBRICK

DON'T PANIC
THERE'S MORE TO COME. . .
DO NOT FEED THE BIRDS

POST CARD.

ADDRESS TO BE WRITTEN HERE.

Mum, Dad and the FREAK,

Finished in OZ. Quality place. Babes surrounding THE STEVENATOR like penguins at feeding time. Already so over Lucy it's untrue. Was flying back to the UK when . . . BOOM! Volcano. Ash cloud. Plane stuck in Thailand!

AWESOME NEWS!

OK, not great news for some people, but hey hey – free holiday!!! In fact, cos I said I'd stay here a few days, the airline gave me FREE money!

SUCKERS!

Laters,

THE STEVENATOR

Mikey – Really looking forward to seeing you. Can't wait.

The Swarbricks
24 Belleview Court
Nelson Avenue
Preston
PR3 5EZ

WELCOME
TO
LAS VEGAS
NEVADA

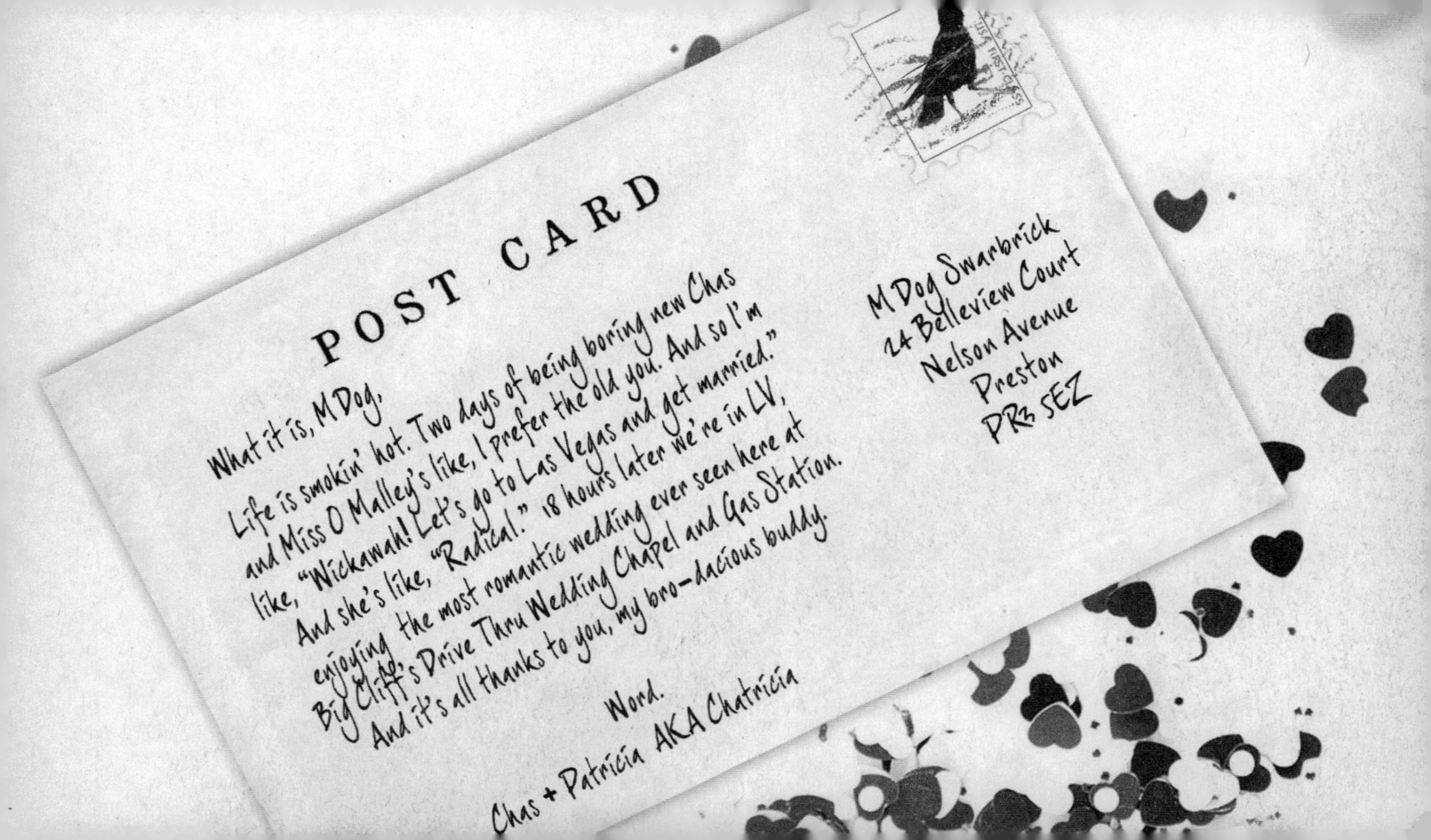

POST CARD

What it is, MDog,
Life is smokin' hot. Two days of being boring new Chas and Miss O'Malley's like, I prefer the old you. And so I'm like, "Wickawah! Let's go to Las Vegas and get married."
And she's like, "Radical." 18 hours later we're in LV, enjoying the most romantic wedding ever seen here at Big Cliff's Drive Thru Wedding Chapel and Gas Station.
And it's all thanks to you, my bro-dacious buddy.
Word.
Chas + Patricia AKA Chatricia

MDog Swarbrick
24 Belleview Court
Nelson Avenue
Preston
PR3 5EZ

GREETINGS FROM PRESTON

Bonjour Chantelle, my sweet soufflé,

I've not stopped thinking of you for un second, since that moment romantique when we kissed goodbye outside the kebab shop at Preston Bus Station. I hope the kebab I bought you was still warm when you got back to France. I thought it would be a nice surprise for when you opened your suitcase – un taste d'angleterre – so I slipped it in there when you weren't looking. Sorry I picked out most of the meat but I'd been waiting there for un grand time.

All my amour, ma petit chou,

Paul

Chantelle Caseau
Rue de St Augustin
Nimes
FRANCE 34332

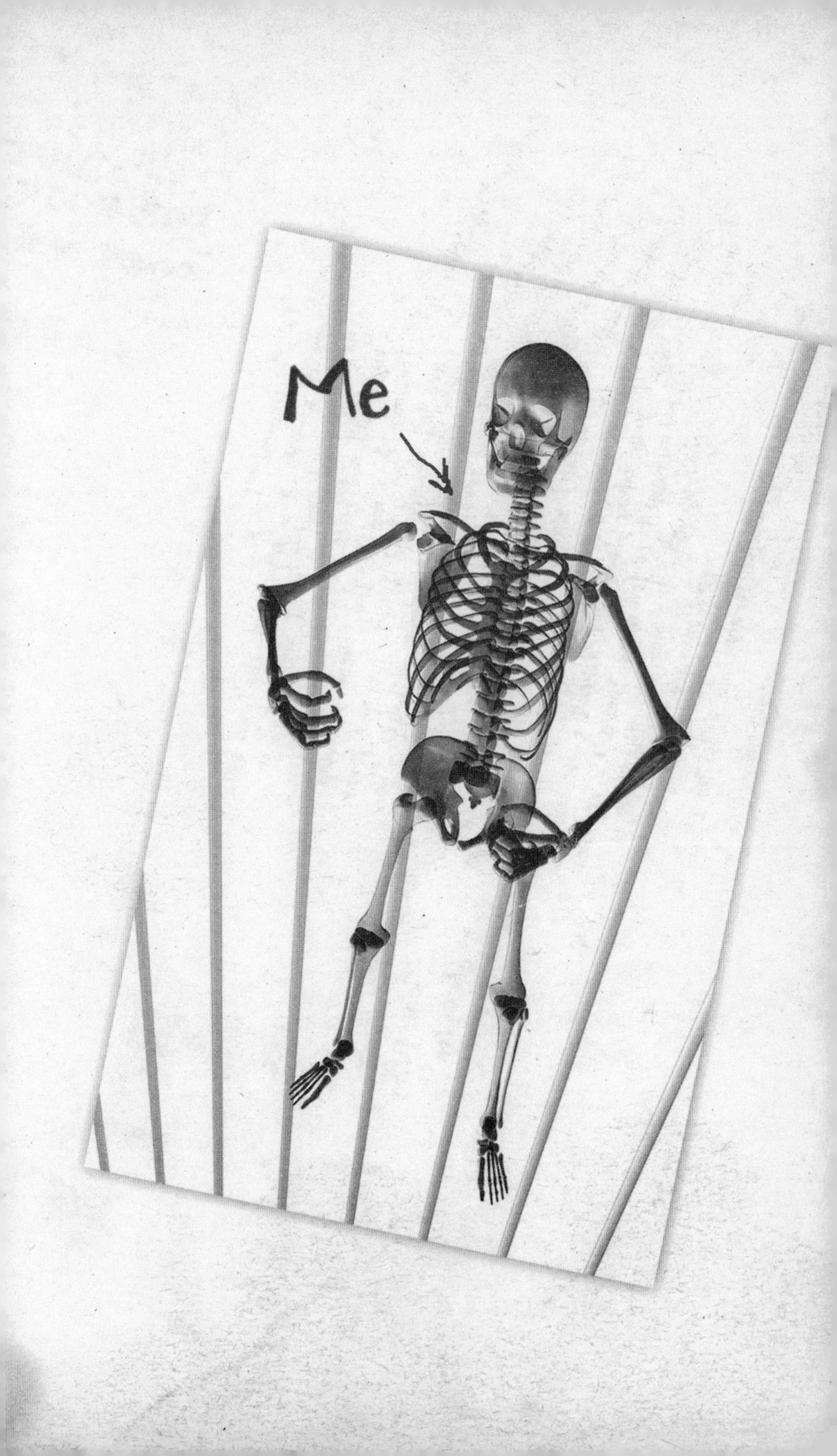
Me

LOOK OUT FOR BOOK
COMING IN 201

To My Dearest Lucy,
I am so sorry. It is my fault that we both got arrested. Had I kept my watch on, we would not have kept the donkey for too long. And maybe the policeman would have let us off had I not emerged from the sea completely naked, although the donkey's overreaction to seeing my body did not help. It did not need to rear up like that. And as for when it tried to kick me, that was completely OTT. Mostly I am sorry about Paul spying on you in your bikini, though. I do not know how he managed to follow us there. Or how he got up into the pier like that. He is a menace.

Please forgive me, Michael x

Lucy King
27 Mede Road
Preston
PR4 2PV

1ST